PRAISE FOR *ALL IN*

"The rules of the game are changing. . . . Hold on for a sexy and thrilling ride through the streets of London as Raine Miller does it again with *All In*."

—TOTALLYBOOKED BLOG

"The Blackstone Affair—Raw. Sensual. Exposed. Surrender to Raine Miller as she draws you *ALL IN*."

—FLIRTY AND DIRTY BOOK BLOG

"*All In* is a must-read! Ethan and Brynne just got hotter!"

—SUGAR AND SPICE BOOK REVIEWS

"You may as well read this one commando, because Ethan's point of view will blow your panties off!"

—SCANDALICIOUS BOOK REVIEWS

"*All In* is a full-course, emotionally charged, gripping read that had me hooked."

—BOOK SAVVY BABE

"Miller's voice is compelling as she tells the tale of these two unlikely lovers. I am *All In* for this series."

—THE INDULGENT BLOGGERS

"A deeply sensual romance with a suspenseful storyline that left me breathless with nearly each page. *All In* is a fabulous read!"

—MY SECRET ROMANCE

ALSO BY RAINE MILLER

Naked: The Blackstone Affair, Book 1

All In

THE BLACKSTONE AFFAIR
BOOK 2

RAINE MILLER

ATRIA PAPERBACK

New York • London • Toronto • Sydney • New Delhi

ATRIA PAPERBACK
A Division of Simon & Schuster, Inc.
1230 Avenue of the Americas
New York, NY 10020

First Atria Paperback edition June 2013

ATRIA PAPERBACK and colophon are trademarks of Simon & Schuster, Inc.

For information about special discounts for bulk purchases, please contact Simon & Schuster Special Sales at 1-866-506-1949 or business@simonandschuster.com.

The Simon & Schuster Speakers Bureau can bring authors to your live event. For more information or to book an event contact the Simon & Schuster Speakers Bureau at 1-866-248-3049 or visit our website at www.simonspeakers.com.

Manufactured in the United States of America

10 9 8 7 6 5 4 3 2 1

Library of Congress Cataloging-in-Publication Data

Miller, Raine.
All in : the Blackstone Affair, book 2 / Raine Miller.
First Atria Books trade paperback edition.
p. cm. — (Blackstone Affair ; 2)
1. Romantic suspense fiction. I. Title.
PS3613.I547A79 2013
813'.6—dc23   2012049355

ISBN 978-1-4767-3527-6
ISBN 978-1-4767-3528-3 (ebook)

For you, Brynne. *You* made this possible.

. . . and I
Have lost the wager. Boldness be my friend!
Arm me, audacity.

—WILLIAM SHAKESPEARE, *CYMBELINE*, 1.6

Acknowledgments

♣ ♠ ♥ ♦

This little story called the Blackstone Affair has taken on quite a life of its own over the months. It's grown and grown into something I never dreamed it would become when I sat down one summer evening, right before the Olympics were starting in London, and began writing about an American nude model and the Englishman who bought her portrait. That little story has without a doubt changed my life and the course of what I'll be doing with my days full-time from here on out. I'm a writer now. I can say that and know it's really true.

I know whom I have to thank for it too.

To all of the fans of the Blackstone Affair who've bought the book and pimped it like mad on their blogs and in their book clubs, to their coworkers, friends, sisters, mothers, grandmothers and even a few husbands, I am eternally grateful. It's only because of you guys that this story took off and flew. THANK YOU from the bottom of my heart.

To all the bloggers who took the advance reading copy and read it early, and gave their feedback, I LOVE YOU. You are the reason I can stay home and be a full-time writer.

In writing this second part of the series, I faced some new challenges. *All In* is Ethan's story. It is the narrative of a British man the whole way through, and while I knew it was how I wanted to write the book, I didn't completely have a grasp of what it meant to do that until I was into it. Well, guess what? I learned fast! I am, after all, an American woman. *snicker* So, to Gitte and Jenny at TotallyBooked, I have one ginormous thank-you to you two girls, for your guidance and knowledge of the Queen's English, and also for the not-so-proper British slang that I used much more of in this story. *wink* I never would have managed it without your help!

So now it's onward with the series, to book 3, *Eyes Wide Open*.

Who knows where it will eventually lead in the future. Such is the magic of the written word.

—*Raine*

All In

THE BLACKSTONE AFFAIR

BOOK 2

Prologue

2012 June
London

I left Ethan at the elevators begging me not to go. It was the hardest thing I'd had to do in a long time. But leave him I did. I'd opened my heart up to Ethan and gotten it stomped. I'd heard him when he told me he loved me and I'd heard him when he'd said he was only trying to protect me from my past. I'd heard him loud and clear. But it didn't change the fact that I needed to get away from him.

All I can envision is the same terrifying idea over and over again.

Ethan knows.

But things are not always what they seem. Impressions are made without full disclosure. Ideas are formed based on emotion and not on factual events. Such was the case with Ethan and me. I found this out later, of course, and in time, when I could back away from the events that had shaped me, I was able to see things a bit differently.

With Ethan everything was fast, intense . . . combustive. From the beginning, he told me things. He told me that he wanted me. And yes, he even said he loved me. He had no problem telling me about what he wanted with me, or how he felt about me. And I don't just mean the sex. That was a big part of our connection, but it wasn't everything with Ethan. He can share his feelings easily. It is his way—not necessarily mine.

I felt like Ethan wanted to consume me at times. He overwhelmed me from the first and was definitely a demanding lover, but one thing was certain—I wanted everything he'd ever given me.

I found that out once I left him.

Ethan gave me some peace and security in a way I'd never really felt as an adult, and certainly never before in regards to my sexuality. It's just how he is, and I think I understand him now. He wasn't demanding and controlling because he wanted to dominate me, he was that way with me because he knew it was what *I* needed. Ethan was trying to give me something I needed in order to make *us* work.

So while those days without him were agonizing, the solitude was critical for me. Our passionate fire had burned white-hot, and we'd both been burned by the heat that sparked and raged so easily when we were together. I know the healing time was necessary for me, but it didn't make the painful ache hurt any less.

I kept coming back to the same idea I had when I'd first found out what he was doing.

Ethan knows what happened to me and there is no way he could possibly love me now.

Chapter 1

My hand throbbed along with my heartbeat. All I could do was breathe at the now sealed doors of the lift that was taking her away from me.

Think for one moment!

Chasing after her was not an option, so I left the lobby and went into the break room. Elaina was in getting coffee. She kept her head down and pretended I wasn't there. Smart woman. I hope those idiots on the floor do the same or they just might need to find new jobs.

I threw some ice into a plastic bag and shoved my hand inside. Fuck, it stung! There was blood on my knuckles and I'm certain on the wall next to the lift. I walked back out to my office with my hand in the ice. I told Frances to call maintenance to come and fix the bloody ding in the wall.

Frances nodded without missing a beat and looked at the bag of ice at the end of my arm. "Do you need an X-ray for that?" she asked, her expression like that of a mum. What I envisioned a mother would look like, at least. I barely remember mine, so I'm probably merely projecting with her.

"No." *I need my girl back, not some fucking X-ray!*

I went through to my office and shut myself in. I pulled out a bottle of Van Gogh from the bar fridge and cracked it. Opening my desk drawer, I fumbled for the pack of Djarum Blacks and the lighter I liked to keep in there. I'd been plowing through the smokes at a record pace since meeting Brynne. I'd have to remember to stock up.

Now all I needed was a glass for the vodka, or maybe not. The bottle would do me just fine. I took a swig with my busted hand and welcomed the pain.

Fuck my hand; it's my heart that's broken.

I stared at her picture. The one I took of her at work when she showed me the painting of Lady Percival with the book. I remembered how I'd used my mobile to take the photo and was pleasantly surprised to see how nice it came out. So nice, in fact, I downloaded it and ordered a print for my office. Didn't matter it was only the camera in a cellular phone— Brynne looked beautiful through any lens. Especially the lenses of my eyes. Sometimes it almost hurt to look at her.

I recalled that morning with her. I could just see her in my mind's eye—how happy she was when I snapped the photo of her smiling down at that old painting . . .

·　　·　　·

I had parked in the lot for the Rothvale Gallery and shut off the engine. It was a dreary day, drizzling and chilly, but not inside my car. Having Brynne sitting next to me, dressed for work, looking beautiful, sexy, smiling at me, had me soaring, but knowing what we'd just shared together that morning was the fucking bomb. And I wasn't talking about the fucking. Remembering the shower and what we'd done there would hold me throughout my day—just barely, but it was knowing that I'd see her again tonight, that we'd be together, that she was mine, and that I could take her to bed and show her all over again. It was the conversation we'd had too. I felt like she'd finally let me in a little. That she cared about me in the same way I cared about her. And it was time to start talking future with us. I wanted so much with her.

"Did I ever tell you how much I like it when you smile at me, Ethan?"

"No," I answered, dropping the smile, "tell me."

She shook her head at my tactics and looked out the window at the rain. "I've always felt special when you do because I think you don't smile much in public. I would describe you as reserved. So when you smile at me I'm kind of . . . swept away."

"Look at me." I waited for her to respond, knowing it would come. This was another thing we had yet to discuss but was crystal clear from the very beginning. Brynne was naturally submissive to me. She accepted what I wanted to give her—the dom in me had found my muse, and it was just one more reason we were perfect together.

I sweep you away, huh?

She lifted her brown/green/gray eyes to me and waited

while my cock pounded in my trousers. I could take her right here in the car and still want her minutes later. She was that much of an addiction.

"Christ, you're beautiful when you do that."

"Do what, Ethan?"

I tucked a strand of her silky hair behind her ear and smiled for her again. "Never mind. You just make me happy, is all. I love bringing you to your job after I've had you all night."

She blushed at me and I wanted to fuck her again.

No, that's not right. I wanted to make love to her … slowly. I could just picture her gorgeous body stretched out naked for me to pleasure in every way I could manage it. *All mine.* For me alone. Brynne made me feel everything—

"Would you like to come in and see what I'm working on? Do you have time?"

I brought her hand to my lips and breathed the scent of her skin. "I thought you'd never ask. Lead on, Professor Bennett."

She laughed. "Someday, maybe. I'll wear one of those black robes and glasses and do my hair up in a bun. I'll give lectures on proper conserving techniques, and you can sit in the back and distract me with inappropriate comments and leering."

"Ahhh, and will you summon me to your office for chastisement then? Will you detain me, Professor Bennett? I am sure we can negotiate a deal for me *working off* my disrespectful behavior." I put my head down toward her lap.

"You are insane," she told me, giggling and pushing me back. "Let's go inside."

We ran through the rain together, my umbrella shielding

us, her slim shape tucked against me, smelling of flowers and sunshine and making me feel like the luckiest man on the planet.

She introduced me to the old security guard, who was clearly in love with her, and led me back into a great, studiolike room. Wide tables and easels were set up with good lighting and plenty of open space. She brought me up to a large oil painting of a dark-haired, solemn woman with startling blue eyes, holding a book.

"Ethan, please say hello to Lady Percival. Lady Percival, my boyfriend, Ethan Blackstone." She smiled at the painting like they were best friends.

I offered a half bow to the painting and said, "My lady."

"Isn't she amazing?" Brynne asked.

I studied the image pragmatically. "Well, she is an arresting figure, to be sure. She looks like she has a story behind her blue eyes." I peered closer to look at the book she held with the front visible. The words were hard to read, but once I realized they were French it was somewhat easier.

"I've been working on the section with the book in particular," Brynne said. "She suffered some heat damage in a fire decades ago, and it's been a struggle getting the cooked-on lacquer off that book. It's special, I just know it."

I looked again and made out the word *Chrétien*. "It's in French. That is the name Christian right there." I pointed.

Her eyes got big and her voice excited. "It is?"

"Yes. And I'm sure this says *Le Conte du Graal.* The Story of the Grail?" I looked at Brynne and shrugged. "The woman in the painting is called Lady Percival, right? Isn't Percival the knight who found the Holy Grail in the King Arthur legend?"

"Good God, Ethan!" She grabbed my arm in excitement. "Of course! Percival . . . it's her story. You figured it out! Lady Percival is holding a very rare book indeed. I *knew* it was something special! One of the first King Arthur stories ever written down; all the way back in the twelfth century. That book is Chrétien de Troyes's *The Story of Perceval and the Grail*." She gazed at the painting, her face glowing with happiness and pure joy, and I reached for my mobile and snapped a picture of her. A magnificent profile shot of Brynne smiling at her Lady Percival.

"Well, I'm glad I could help you, baby."

She leapt at me and kissed me on the lips, her arms wrapped tightly around me. It was the most amazing feeling in the world.

"You did! You helped me so much. I'm going to call the Mallerton Society today and tell them what you discovered. They will be interested, I'm sure. There's his birthday exhibit coming next month . . . I wonder if they'll want to include this."

Brynne rambled, excitedly telling me everything I could ever have wanted to know about rare books, paintings of rare books, and the conserving of paintings of rare books. Her face flushed with the thrill of solving a mystery, but that smile and kiss were worth their weight in gold to me.

I opened my eyes and tried to get my bearings. My head felt like I'd been smashed with a board. A half-empty bottle of Van Gogh stared at me. Djarum butts were sprinkled atop my desk where my cheek was stuck fast, filling my nose with the scent of stale cloves and tobacco. I peeled my face off the desktop and propped my head in my hands, supported on firmly planted elbows.

The same desk where I'd laid her out and fucked her only a few hours before. Yes, fucked. That had been pure, unapologetic shagging, and so good my eyes stung at the remembrance. The light on my mobile blinked madly. I flipped it over so I didn't have to look. I knew none of the calls were from her anyway.

Brynne wouldn't call me. Of that I was certain. The only question was how long before I tried calling her.

It was nighttime now. Dark outside. Where was she? Was she horribly hurt and upset? Crying? Being comforted by her friends? Hating me? Yeah, probably all of those, and I couldn't go to her and make it better either. *She doesn't want you.*

So this is what it feels like. Being in love. It was time to face some truths about Brynne and what I'd done to her. So I stayed in my office and faced it. I couldn't go home. There was too much of her there already, and seeing her things would only drive me utterly mad. I'd stay here tonight and sleep on sheets that didn't have her scent all over them. *Didn't have her in them.* A wave of panic sliced into me and I had to move.

I heaved my arse off the chair and stood up. I saw the scrap of pink fabric on the floor at my feet and knew what it was. The lacy knickers I'd peeled off her during that session on my desk.

Fuck! Remembering where I was when that message from her dad came through. *Buried inside her.* It was agonizing to touch something that had last been against her skin. I fingered the fabric and put them in my pocket. A shower was calling my name.

I went through the back door to the attached suite set up with a bed, a bath, a TV and a small kitchen—everything top of the line. The perfect bachelor crash pad for the busy professional man who works so late there's no point in driving home.

Or more like a fuck pad. This is where I brought women if I wanted to fuck them. Always after hours, of course, and they never stayed the whole night. I got my "dates" the hell out long before dawn. All of this was before I found Brynne. I never wanted to bring her here. She was different from the beginning. Special. *My beautiful American girl.*

Brynne didn't even know about this suite. She would have figured it out in two seconds flat and hated me for bringing her into it. I rubbed my chest and tried to still the ache that burned. I turned on the shower and got undressed.

As the hot water poured over me, I leaned against the tile and faced exactly where I was. *You're not with her! You made a cock-up of everything, and she doesn't want you now.*

My Brynne had left me for the second time. The first time she did it in stealth in the middle of the night because she was terrorized by a bad dream. This time she just turned and walked away from me without looking back. I could see it in her face, and it wasn't fear that made her leave. It was utter devastation at the betrayal, to find I had kept the truth from her. I had broken her trust. I'd wagered too high and lost.

The urge to pull her back and make her stay was so great I punched the wall and likely fractured something to keep from grabbing her. She told me never to contact her again.

I turned off the shower and stepped out, the desolate sounds of dripping water draining away, making my chest hurt worse from the hollowness. I pulled down a plush towel and shoved my head in it. I stared at my image in the mirror as my face was revealed. Naked, wet and miserable. Alone. I realized another truth as I stared at my motherfucker asshole self.

Never is a very long time. I might be able to give her a day or two, but *never* was irrefutably out of the question.

The fact that she still needed protection from a threat which could prove dangerous hadn't changed either. I couldn't allow anything to happen to the woman I love. *Never*.

I smiled into the mirror, my cleverness amusing even me in my sorry state, for I had just found a perfect example of the proper usage for the word *never*.

Chapter 2

♣ ♠ ♥ ♦

Day two of my exile from Brynne and it sucked. I was moving around and doing things, but nothing felt right. How long would I be like this? Should I call her? If I thought about my situation too much, dread started to creep in, so I left it alone. I left her alone. The empty space inside me pushed for action, but I knew it was too soon to try to go to her. She needed some time, and I'd made this mistake before. Pressing too fast and too hard with her. *And being an utter selfish prick.*

I parked on the street next to the house where I'd grown up. The lawn very tidy, the gate straight and the shrubbery clipped as it had always been. Dad would never leave here. Not the home where he'd been with my mother. My dad gave the term *stubborn old man* new meaning, and this was where he would die someday.

I picked the cold beer off the seat and went in through the gate. A black cat dashed ahead of me and waited. It was not quite a kitten and not fully grown either. A teenage cat, I suppose. It sat down right in front of the door, then turned and looked at me. Bright green eyes blinked as if saying for me to hurry up my too-slow arse and let him in the house. When in the hell had Dad gotten a cat?

I rang the bell, then opened the door and stuck my head in. "Dad?" The cat slithered into the house faster than the speed of light and all I could do was stare. "You have a cat now?" I called out and went into the kitchen. I put the beer in the fridge and flopped on the couch.

Remote pointed, I turned on the box. European championship. *Fucking perfect.* I could focus on football for a few hours, hopefully drink four out of the six beers and forget about my girl for a little while. *And cry to my dad.*

I leaned my head back and closed my eyes. Something furry and soft climbed into my lap. The cat was back.

"Ahh, well, you're here then, and I see you've met Soot." My dad walked up behind me.

"Why did you get a cat?" I couldn't wait for this answer. We'd never had cats growing up.

My dad snorted and sat down in his chair. "I didn't. You could say that he got me."

"I can imagine." I stroked my hand down Soot's sleek body. "He just came in the house the second I opened the front door like he owned the place."

"My neighbor asked me to feed him while she left to take

care of her mum, who's very ill. She's had to move into her mother's house and I got him by default. We have an understanding, I s'pose."

"You and the neighbor, or you and the cat?"

My dad looked at me shrewdly, his eyes narrowing. Jonathan Blackstone was very perceptive by nature. Always had been. I could never slip anything by him. He always knew if I came home drunk and when I started smoking, or if I was into trouble as a lad. I guess he'd been that way because he was a single parent for most of our lives. My sister, Hannah, and I were never neglected despite the loss of our mum. His senses got keener and he could sniff out problems like a bloodhound. He was doing it now.

"What the hell happened to you, son?"

Brynne happened.

"That noticeable, huh?" The cat started purring in my lap.

"I know my own child and I know when something's off with you." My dad left the room for a minute. He returned with two of the beers opened and handed me one. "Mexican beer?" He lifted an eyebrow at me, and I wondered if I looked the same way when I did it. Brynne had remarked on my eyebrow quirking more than once.

"Yeah. It's good with a sliver of lime shoved down the neck." I took a slug and stroked my new ebony friend. "It's a girl. Brynne. I met her, and I fell for her, and now she's left me." Short and sweet. What else was there to say to my own father? This was all that mattered or all that I could think about. I was aching for her and she had left me.

"Ahhh, well, that makes more sense." Dad paused for a moment as if letting it all sink in. I am sure he was surprised by the revelation. "My lad, I know I've told you before, so this is not news by any stretch, but you came to your good looks from your mum, rest her soul. All you got from me was the name and maybe my bulk. And your blessings in the Adonis department made it very easy for you with the ladies."

"I've never chased women, Dad."

"I didn't say you did, but the point is you never had to. They chased you." He shook his head in remembrance. "Gods, you had the females clamoring for you. I was sure you'd get caught sowing your oats and make me a granddad long before you should have done." He gave me a look that suggested he'd spent much more time worrying about this than he'd wanted to. "But you never did . . ." Dad trailed off and got a rather sad look in his eye. After school I'd shipped off to the military and left home. *And nearly didn't come back . . .*

Dad patted my knee and took a pull on his beer.

"I never wanted anyone like I want her." I shut my mouth and started in earnest on the beer. Someone scored a goal in the game and I forced myself to watch and pet the cat.

Dad was patient for a while, but he got his questions in eventually. "What did you do that made her leave you?"

It hurt just to hear the question. "I lied. It was a lie of omission, but still I didn't tell her the truth and she found out." I set the cat off my lap carefully and went into the kitchen for another beer. I brought back two instead.

"Why did you lie to her, son?"

I met my dad's dark eyes and spoke something I'd never said before. It had never been true before. "Because I love her. I love her and didn't want to scare her by bringing up a painful memory of the past."

"So you've gone and fallen in love." He nodded his head knowingly and looked me over. "Well, you've got all the signs. I should have realized when you showed up here looking like you'd slept under a bridge."

"She left me, Dad." I started on the next beer and pulled the cat back onto my lap.

"You've said that already." Dad spoke dryly and kept looking me over like I might not be his son at all but some alien impostor. "So why did you lie to the woman you love? Best to tell it, Ethan."

It's my dad and I trust him with my life. I am sure there is no other person I *could* tell, apart from possibly my sister. I took a deep breath and told him.

"I met Brynne's father, Tom Bennett, at a poker tournament in Las Vegas years ago. We hit it off and he was good at cards. Not as good as me, but we developed a friendship. He contacted me recently and asked a favor. I wasn't going to do it. I mean, look at what's on my plate at the moment with work. I can't provide protection for an American art student slash model when I have to organize VIP security for the fucking Olympics!"

The cat flinched. Dad merely raised a brow and got comfy in his chair. "But you did," he said.

"Yeah, I did. I got a look at the picture he sent me and I was curious. Brynne does modeling on the side and she is . . . so beautiful." I wish I had her portrait in my house already. But the conditions for purchase were that it stayed on display at the Andersen Gallery for six months.

My dad just looked at me and waited.

"So I arrive at this gallery show and buy a damn portrait

of her within a few moments of seeing it, like a sodding poet or something! As soon as I met her I was ready to send in the guard to keep her safe if need be." I shook my head. "What the hell happened to me, Dad?"

"Your mother loved to read all the poets. Keats, Shelley, Byron." He smiled just slightly. "It happens that way sometimes. You find the one for you and that's all there is to it. Men have been falling in love with women since time began, son. You just finally made it to the head of the queue." Dad took another drink of his beer. "Why does . . . Brynne need protection?"

"That U.S. congressman who died in the plane crash has got a replacement. Name is Senator Oakley from California. Well, the senator has a son, one Lance Oakley, who used to date Brynne. There was some trouble . . . and a sex tape—" I paused and realized how horrible it must sound to my dad. "But she was a very young girl—only seventeen—and terribly hurt by the betrayal. Oakley was a right prick to her. She sees a therapist . . ." I trailed off, wondering how my dad was taking all this in. I drank some more beer before telling the last part. "The son got shipped off to Iraq and Brynne came to study at University of London. She studies art and conserves paintings, and she's absolutely brilliant at it."

Dad surprised me by not reacting to all the ugliness I'd just told. "I am assuming that the senator does not want publicity about his badly behaving son to hit the news." He looked annoyed. My dad hates politicians, no matter their nationality.

"The senator and the powerful party that's backing him. Something like this will lose them the election."

"What about the opposing party? They'll be looking for it as hard as Oakley's people are trying to bury it," my dad said.

I shook my head in question. "Why are you not working for me, Dad? You get it. You can see the bigger picture. I need about ten of you, though," I said wryly.

"Ha! I'm very happy to help when you need me, but I'm not doing it for pay."

"Yeah, I am very aware of that," I said, holding up one hand. I'd tried to get him to come and work for me for a long time, and it was sort of a joke between us. He never would accept any money, though—stubborn old fool that he was.

"Has anything happened to suggest that your Brynne needs protection? Seems a bit alarmist, really. Why did her father ask you?"

"The senator's son is still finding trouble, it seems. He was home on leave, and one of his mates got killed in an altercation at a bar. More loud noise that politicians hate for a reason. It causes digging into places they don't want people to know about. Could just be an isolated incident, but the friend knew about the video. Brynne's dad went on full alert at that point. In his words, 'When the people who know about that video start turning up dead, then I need to protect my daughter.'" I shrugged. "He asked me to help him. I said no initially and offered a referral to another firm, but he sent me her picture in an email."

"And you couldn't say no after you'd seen her picture." Dad worded it as a statement. I knew then that he understood how I felt about Brynne.

"No. I could not." I shook my head. "I was mesmerized. I went to the gallery show and bought her portrait. And when she came into the room, Dad, I couldn't take my eyes off her. She intended to walk to the Tube in the dark, so I introduced myself and convinced her to let me take her home in my car. I tried to leave her alone after that. I really wanted to . . ."

He smiled again. "You've always been a protective lad."

"But it became so much more for me than just a job. I want to be with Brynne . . ." I looked over at my father sitting quietly and listening, his big body still fit for a man of sixty-three. I knew that he understood. I didn't need to explain any more about my motivations, and that part was a relief.

"But she found out that her father hired you to protect her?"

"Yes. She overheard a telephone call in my office. Her dad exploded when he realized we were seeing each other and challenged me on it." I figured my dad might as well know the whole bloody mess.

"She felt betrayed and exposed, I imagine, if her past with the senator's son, or whomever, is something that you know and didn't tell her you knew." Dad shook his head. "What were you thinking? And she should be told about the death of that other bloke—about the possibility of a threat toward her. *And* that you love her. And that you intend to still keep her safe. A woman needs the truth, son. You'll have to tell her everything if you want her to trust you again."

"I did tell her." I blew out a huge sigh and leaned my head back on the couch to look at the ceiling. Soot stretched and rearranged himself in my lap.

"Well, try harder, then. Start with the truth and go from there. She will either accept you or she won't. But you don't have to give up, either. You can keep trying."

I took out my mobile, pulled up the picture of Brynne looking at the painting and held it out for him. He smiled as he studied her image through his glasses. A reminiscent suggestion in his eyes told me he was thinking of my mother. He handed it back after a moment.

"She's a lovely girl. I hope we get the chance to meet someday." Dad looked me straight in the eye and told me like it is. No sympathy, just the brutal truth. "You'll have to follow your heart, son . . . nobody can do that for you."

I left my dad's place later in the afternoon, went home and worked out for three hours in my gym. I kept at it until I was nothing but a quivering mass of aching muscles and sweaty stink. The bubbly soak in my tub after was nice, though. And the smokes. I smoked too much now. It wasn't good for me and I needed to tone it down. But fuck, the urge was strong. Being with Brynne had soothed me enough so I didn't crave it as much, but now that she'd left, I was chain-smoking like the serial killer we'd joked about in our very first conversation.

I hung the Djarum off my lip and stared down at the bubbles.

Brynne loved taking baths. She didn't have a tub at her flat, and she told me she missed it. I loved the idea of her naked in my bathtub. *Her naked . . .* This was something that did me absolutely no good to think about, yet I'd spent many hours doing it. And, if I reasoned why, was the basis for everything that'd happened with us. *Her naked . . .* That photograph Tom Bennett sent to me was the same one I bought at the show. From a pragmatic view it was just a picture of a beautiful naked body anyone would appreciate, male or female. But even with the little he told me in the beginning, paired with that picture of her in all its vulnerability, allure and stark beauty, the thought she could be in danger or that someone would purposefully hurt her galvanized me to go out to the street and get her safely into my car. I just couldn't walk away from her and keep my conscience intact. And once we'd met my mind went mad with fantasies. All I could see in my head while we talked was . . . *her naked*.

My bath started losing its heat after a bit and, understandably, its appeal. So I got out and dressed and went in search of the book. *Letters of John Keats to Fanny Brawne*.

Something Dad mentioned reminded me of it. He'd said my mother loved reading the great poets. I knew Brynne loved Keats. I'd found the book on the sofa, where she'd obviously been reading, and asked her about it. Brynne had confessed her love for him and wanted to know why I even had the book in my house. I told her that my dad was always giving me books that people left behind in his cab. He hated to toss them out, so he would bring them home whenever he acquired anything decent. When I'd bought my flat, he'd hauled over a few boxes of books to fill the shelves, and it must have been in the lot. I truthfully told her I'd never read any Keats.

I was reading now.

Keats had a way with words, I was discovering. For a man who died at only twenty-five, he sure packed some emotion into his letters to his girlfriend when they were apart. And I could feel his pain like it was my own. It *was* my own.

I decided to write her a letter using a pen and paper. I found some nice cotton stationery in my office and took the book with me. Simba flickered his fins from the aquarium when I walked up, always expecting a treat. I am a sucker for begging animals, so I dropped in a freeze-dried krill and watched him devour it.

"She loves you, Simba. Maybe if I tell her that you are pining and off your feed she'll come back." So I was talking to fish now. How in the hell had I got to this lowly point? I ignored the urge for a cigarette, washed my hands and sat down to write.

Brynne,

"I do not know how elastic my spirit might be, what pleasure I might have in living here if the remembrance of you did not weigh so upon me. Ask yourself my love whether you are not very cruel to have so entrammeled me, so destroyed my freedom.

. . . All my thoughts, my unhappiest days and nights have, I find not at all cured me of my love of Beauty, but made it so intense that I am miserable that you are not with me . . . I cannot conceive of any beginning of such love I have for you but Beauty." July 1819

I know you will recognize the words of Keats. I started reading the book you like. I can say I have an understanding now of what the man was trying to express to Miss Brawne about how she had captured his heart.

Like you've captured my heart, Brynne.

I miss you. Thoughts of you never leave me, and if I can say it once more and have you believe me, then I guess there is some comfort in that. I can only try to make you know what I feel.

I am immensely sorry for keeping my knowledge of your past and how I came to notice you a secret, but you need to know something, because it's the brutal truth. I had no intentions of taking the job. I planned to give your father the name of another agency to secure you. I couldn't do that, though, as soon as I met you. I wanted to tell you that night on the street that your father was trying to arrange protection, but when I saw how you looked at me, Brynne, I felt something—a connection with you. Things moved inside me and clicked into place. The missing piece of my puzzle? I don't know what it was, I just know it happened to me the night we met. I tried to keep a distance and let you slip away back into your life, but I couldn't do it. I was drawn to you from the first moment I saw your portrait. I had to know you. And then to be with you. To have you look at me and really see me. I know now that I fell in love. I fell in love with a beautiful American girl. You, Brynne.

There were many times I wanted to say how I came to find you that night at the gallery. I stopped myself every time because I was afraid of hurting you. I could see how haunted you were when you woke up with the nightmare. I could only guess as to why, but I would do anything to keep you from being hurt. I knew somehow that telling you your dad hired security to protect you from powerful political enemies would scare the hell out of you. It scares the hell out of me to think of anyone targeting you for harm, emotional or otherwise. I know you said I was fired, but if anything happens or somebody frightens you, I want you to call me and

I will come to you in a moment. I am deadly serious about this. Call me.

You are someone so very special, Brynne. I feel things with you—emotions and ideas and dreams; a deep understanding that brings me to a place I never thought I'd find with another person. But I have demons too. I am terrified of facing them without you. I don't know what I'm doing most of the time but I do know how I feel about you. And even if you hate me for what I did, I'll still love you. If you won't see me, I'll still love you. I'll still love you because you are mine. Mine, Brynne. In my heart you are, and nobody can take that away from me. Not even you.

E

A week passed before I sent Brynne my letter. Longest fucking week of my life.

Not exactly true, but I'd smoked enough Djarums to either bankrupt me or give me cancer. I told the florist purple flowers and to include the letter. It was Sunday afternoon when I ordered them, and the florist told me they would be delivered on Monday. I had them sent to her at work instead of her flat. I knew she'd been busy with school and wanted to wait until her final exams were over and finished.

Brynne and I are not over and finished. This is the mantra I continued to tell myself during those days because it was the only option I could accept.

Chapter 3

♣ ♠ ♥ ♦

They make you believe things that are not true. They tell you so many times, you accept what they are telling you *is* the truth rather than lies. You suffer for it like it's the truth. The most effective torture is not physical—it is mental of course. The mind can imagine terrors far more horrific than you could ever physically bear, just like the mind will tune out those physical hurts when the pain surpasses what your body can endure.

The nerves in my back screamed like acid had been poured onto the destroyed flesh. The pain took my breath away, it was so acute. I wondered how long till I passed out, and if I did, whether I wake again in this life. I doubted I could walk more than a few yards. I could barely see for the blood in my eyes and blows to the head. I would die here in this hellhole, and probably soon. I hoped it was soon. My dad and Hannah couldn't see me like this, though. I hoped they never found out how I met my end. I prayed there wouldn't be a video of my execution. Please, Christ, no video of that—

Luck of the draw. I'd had no luck when they ambushed our team. No luck when my weapon jammed. No luck when I didn't die trying to evade capture. These fuckers learned their techniques from the Russians. They loved to get Western prisoners. And British SF? I was a fucking crown jewel. And totally expendable to my country. Luck of the draw. A sacrifice for the greater good, for democracy, for free will.

Fuck free will. I had none.

My tormentor this day loved to talk. He never stopped talking about her. I really wish he would shut his filthy hole. They don't know where she is . . . they don't know how to find her . . . they don't even know her name. *I kept telling myself these truths because it is all I have at my disposal to work with.*

The backhand to my face roused me. And then another woke me fully.

"We will make you watch when we take her. She will scream like the whore she is. An American whore who does naked photographs." *He spit in my face and jerked my head back by the hair.* "So disgusting, your women . . . they deserve everything that happens to them. To be used like a dirty whore." *He laughed at me.*

I stared at him and memorized his face. I would never forget it, and if the opportunity arose I would cut out his tongue before I killed him. Even if the killing was simply imagined in my mind.

He did not like my reaction. Inside I was frozen with fear. How could I stop her from being taken? I wanted to beg, but I didn't. I just stared and felt my heart thump inside my chest, verifying my status as alive. For now.

"Every guard will have a turn between her thighs. Then when their lust slackens she may watch when we take your head. You know this will be the way you meet your end, don't you?" He held my neck back and dragged his finger across my throat. "You will be begging for mercy like the pig you are . . . about to be slaughtered. You won't be proud then." He laughed in my face, his yellow teeth flashing. "And then we will kill your American whore in the same way—"

I bolted up in my bed gasping, my hand on my cock and dripping in sweat. I leaned against the headboard and took stock of where I was . . . and thankfully where I wasn't. *You aren't there anymore.* It was just a dream. *That was a long time ago.*

My nightmare was the sort that takes all the bad shit that ever happened to you and stirs it together into a dreadful brew you must bathe in. I closed my eyes in relief. Brynne was not a part of the horror from Afghanistan. She was of the here and now. Brynne lived in London, working and taking her graduate degree. *It was just your subconscious mixing together everything that's bad. Brynne is safe in town.*

She just wasn't with *me* anymore.

I looked down at my cock, hot and hard, and wrapped my fist around the shaft. I closed my eyes and started stroking. If I kept them closed I could remember that day in my office. I needed the release right now. I needed to come so I could stop the bloody shakes invading from that fucked-up nightmare. Whatever worked. It'd be a temporary fix but would have to do.

I remembered. The first time she came to see me at work. She had on red boots and a black skirt. I told her to sit on my lap and made her come with my hand up her quim. *So fucking sexy, showing up in my office.* She looked beautiful falling apart in my arms from what I did to her, from what I made her feel.

Brynne had tried to pull away from me and I didn't want her to. I remember she had to tug herself off my lap. But when she slid to her knees and touched me through my trousers, I understood. She told me she wanted to suck me. I knew I loved her in that moment. I knew because she is honest and generous, with no artifice. She is real and perfect and mine.

Not now, she isn't. She left you.

I kept my eyes closed and remembered the vision of her beautiful lips closing over the bell end of my cock and taking me in. How wet and warm and exquisite her mouth felt that first time. How beautiful the moment when she swallowed and looked up at me in that sexy, mysterious way she has. I never know what she is thinking. She is a woman, after all.

I remembered everything—the sounds she made, her long hair all about her face, the slick slide against her warm lips, the grip on the shaft as she twisted and pulled me deep into her beautiful mouth.

I remembered that special time with Brynne back then, as I jerked myself to an empty climax in my very pathetic and lonely present. I had to remember or I wouldn't have got off. I cried out as the spunk shot out of the top of my cock in a near painful rush, all over the sheets on my bed, shiny white against the black. *It should be her!* I panted against the head-board and let the release spread throughout my body, angered that I'd just wanked off to her image like some desperate freak.

I couldn't care less about the mess. Sheets can be washed. My mind cannot.

I can remember every time I was in her.

The emptiness invading me is something almost cruel, and the climax definitely no substitute for the real thing. Very hollow and utterly useless.

No possible way, Benny! He's far too beautiful to have to resort to his hand for an orgasm.

Yeah, right. I got up and headed for my shower. Nothing but her will ever be enough.

She rang me that afternoon on my mobile. I missed her call because of an idiot meeting. I wanted to hurt the morons who'd taken my time, but I hit voice mail instead.

"Ethan, I—I got your letter." Her voice sounded thready and the urge to go to her was so great I didn't know how I would manage to keep away. "Thanks for sending it. The flowers are beautiful too. I—I just wanted you to know that I talked to my dad and he told me some stuff—"

She lost her composure then. I could hear the sounds of muffled crying. I knew she was, and it broke my heart wide open. "I have to go . . . maybe later we could talk." She whispered the last. "Bye, Ethan." And then she hung up.

I thought I would crack the glass in my mobile punching buttons to redial, praying she picked up and would speak to me. Time slowed down interminably while the call connected. Once, twice, three rings. My heart pounded and the need for air increased—

"Hi." Just one little word. But it was her voice and she was directing it to me. I could hear noises in the background. Like traffic.

"Brynne, how are you? You sounded upset on your message. I was in a meeting . . ." I trailed off, realizing I'd started rambling. I forced my mouth closed and desperately wished for a lovely black clove cigarette.

She breathed heavy into the receiver. "Ethan, you said to call if anything weird happened—"

"What happened? Are you all right? Where are you right now?" I felt my blood run cold at her words and the sound of her voice. "Are you outside?"

"I'm on a run at the moment. I had to get out of my head for a bit and just take a break."

"I'm coming to you. Tell me where you are."

She got quiet. I could hear the cars moving around her and I hated being forced to endure the imagined visualization of where she was at the moment. Alone on the street. Vulnerable. Unprotected.

"Will you tell me, please? I have to see you—we need to talk. And I want to hear what worried you enough to ring me and leave that message earlier." More silence. "Baby, I can't help if you won't let me in."

"Did you see it?" Her voice changed, becoming harsh.

"See what?" I swear I only wanted to go to her and get her in my arms. Her question didn't register at first. The cold silence on the other end helped me figure it out real quick, though.

"Did you watch it, Ethan? Answer my question."

"The sex tape of you and Oakley?"

She made a sound of anguish.

"Fuck no! Brynne . . ." The fact she even asked me such a thing pissed me off. "Why would I do that?"

"It's hardly a sex tape!" she yelled into my ear. My chest ached like a knife had been shoved in.

"Well, that's what your dad told me it was!" I yelled back at her, confused by her questioning and utterly at a loss in this fucked-up conversation we were having. If I could talk to her in person, get close to her, make her look me in the eye and listen, I might have a chance. But this fractured argument was getting us nowhere fast. I tried again in a more reasonable tone. "Brynne, please let me come to where you are."

She was crying again. I could hear the soft sound of her against the fainter sounds of traffic. I did not like that she was out running alone either. Cars on the street speeding by her, men looking at her, indigents bothering her for handouts . . .

"What the hell did he tell you, Ethan? What did my dad say about me?"

"I don't want to do this on the telephone—"

"Tell. Me." And then silence.

I closed my eyes in dread, knowing she wouldn't accept anything but the brutal truth, hating like hell to say it to her, but knowing I had to. How to start? I didn't know any other way than by just jumping in feet first. I sent up a silent prayer to my mum for strength.

"He told me you and Oakley dated in school. When you were seventeen Oakley made a sex video without your knowledge and spread it around. You dropped out of school and had trouble after that. The senator shipped his son off to Iraq and you came here to study and start afresh. Now the senator is trying to win an election as vice president and wants to make sure nobody ever sees the video . . . or hears about it. Your dad told me one of Oakley's mates has died under an unusual circumstance and he's worried people connected to that video may be targeted . . . including you. It concerned him enough that he contacted me and asked a favor—that I look after you and watch for anyone who might approach you."

What I wouldn't give for a cigarette right now. The silence on the other end was painful to bear, but after a few interminable beats I heard the welcome sound of her saying words I wanted to hear. Words I could work with. Something I understood and could do something about. "That scares me."

Relief washed over me, hearing that. Not that she was scared, but that she sounded like she needed me. Like she would let me back in. "I won't let anyone or anything hurt you, baby."

"I got a weird message on my cell phone two days ago. A man. From some newspaper. I didn't know what to do—and then when I got your letter today I—I read what you said about calling you if anyone did something to bother me."

The feeling of relief vanished instantly. "Enough of this shit, Brynne! Where are you right now? I'm coming to get you!" I would have crawled through the fucking mobile if the laws of physics allowed it. I needed to get to her and that was all, period. To hell with the bloody yammering, I had to have Brynne next to me in the flesh where I could put my hands on her.

"I'm at the south end of the Waterloo Bridge."

Of course you are. I rolled my eyes. Just hearing the word *Waterloo* annoyed me. "I'm leaving now. Can you get over to the Victoria Embankment and wait for me there? I can find you quickly that way."

"Okay. I'll go to the sphinx." She sounded better to me. Less afraid, and the feeling did wonders for my stress level. I was going to get my girl. She might not know that yet, but it was in fact the reality of what was about to happen.

"That'll do. If someone approaches you, just keep to the open spaces where there are people about." I kept her on the line as she made her way to Cleopatra's Needle on foot while I drove like a fiend and avoided London's Finest.

"I'm here," she said.

"Are there others around you?"

"Yes. There's a walking tour and some couples and people with their dogs."

"Good. I'm parking now. I'll find you." We ended the call.

My heart pounded in my chest as I found a place to park and started walking down to the embankment. How would this go? Would she resist me? I didn't want to pick at our wounds, but fuck if I'd let this bloody mess go on for another day. It ended now. Today. Whatever it took to fix this cock-up got figured out right here, right now.

The sun was just starting to set when I spotted her. Her track shorts hugged her body like a second skin. She had her back to me as she leaned over the rail to look out at the river, the wind blowing her ponytail to the side, one long leg bent toward the railing with her hands resting gracefully on the top.

I slowed down because I simply wanted to soak in her

image. I was finally looking at her after a week of starvation. Right in front of me. *Brynne.*

I needed my hands on her. They itched to hold her close and touch. But she looked different—slimmer. The nearer I got, the more visible it became. Christ, had she stopped eating in the past week? She must have dropped nearly half a stone. I stopped and stared, anger mixing with concern, but more so understanding that this shit with her past was way bigger than I'd realized up to this point. *Lucky us, we can be fucked up together.*

She turned around and found me. Our eyes connected and some powerful communication flowed through the breeze between us. Brynne knew how I felt. She should know. I'd told her plenty of times. She had never told me what I'd said to her, though. I was still waiting to hear those three words come from her. *I love you.*

She said my name. I read her lips. I couldn't hear the sound through the wind, but I saw that she did indeed speak my name. She looked about as relieved as I felt seeing her in one piece and just a few steps away. And utterly beautiful to me, as she always was and always had been.

But this was where I stopped. If Brynne wanted me, she needed to walk over here and show me how she felt. It would kill me if she didn't, but my dad's advice was spot-on true. Everyone had to follow their heart. I followed mine. Now Brynne needed to do the same.

She stepped off the railing and parts inside me thudded when she paused. Almost like she waited for me to make a gesture or come and get her. *No, baby.* I didn't smile, and neither did she, but we certainly made contact.

She had on a turquoise sports top that hugged her breasts and made me think about her naked and underneath me, my hands and mouth taking her all in. I wanted her so badly I ached. I guess that's what falling in love will do to a person—make you ache in a way for which there is only one cure. Brynne was my cure. Images of her and me making love flashed through my head as I waited for her; the scenes of my desires haunting relentlessly with a craving that burned me from the inside out. I *burned* for Brynne. Mr. Keats sure knew what he was talking about in his poems.

I held out my hand and locked my eyes onto hers, but my feet stayed planted. And then I saw the change. A flicker in her lovely eyes. She understood what I was asking of her. She got it. And again, I was reminded of how good we were together at the most fundamental level. Brynne got me, and that alone made my hunger for her even stronger.

She kept coming until her arm lifted. Closer still until our fingers touched, her smaller, finely formed hand resting in my much bigger one. My fingers wrapped over her wrist and palm in a firm grip and pulled her in the rest of the way. Right up against my chest, body to body. I wrapped my arms around her and buried my head in her hair. The scent I knew and craved was up my nose and in my head again. I had her. I had Brynne again.

I pulled back and took her face in my hands. I held her in that position so I could really look at her. She never wavered with her eyes. My girl was brave. Life sucked at times, but she hung in and didn't shrink away. I looked at her lips and knew I was going to kiss her whether she wanted it or not. I hoped she wanted it.

Her lovely lips were just as soft and sweet as before. More so because I'd been without them for too long. It felt like heaven having my mouth on hers. I sort of got lost in the moment and forgot we were in public. Lost in my Brynne the instant she responded to me.

She kissed me back, and it felt so good to feel her tongue tangling with mine that I groaned against her mouth. I knew what I wanted to do. And my requirements were few. Privacy. Brynne naked. If only things were that simple. I remembered we were standing amid a crowd of humanity on the Victoria Embankment and unfortunately not anywhere near private.

I stopped kissing and brushed over her bottom lip with my thumb. "You'll come with me. Right now."

She nodded into my hands and I kissed her once more. A thank-you kiss.

We didn't talk as we walked to the Rover. We held hands, though. I wasn't letting go until I had to in order to put her in the car. Once she was in the passenger seat and the doors were locked, I turned and really looked at her. She looked half starved, and it made me angry. I remembered the first night we met and how I got her the PowerBar and the water.

"Where are we going?" she asked.

"First? To get you some food." It came out a little harsher than I wanted it to.

She nodded at me and then looked away, out the window.

"After you eat, we'll get a new phone and mobile number for you. I need to have your old one so I can track whoever tries to contact you. All right?"

She looked down at her lap and nodded again. I almost pulled her into my arms and told her everything would be fine, but I held off.

"Then I'm taking you home. My place—*home*."

"Ethan, that's not a good idea," she whispered, still looking down at her lap.

"Fuck good ideas," I exploded. "Would you at least look at me?" She turned her eyes up to mine and smoldered in the seat, a hint of red fire flickering, making them look very brown. I wanted to drag her to me and shake her, force her to understand that this bullshit breakup was a thing of the past. She was coming home with me, period. I turned the key in the ignition.

"What do you want from me, Ethan?"

"That's easy." I made a rude noise. "I want to go back to ten days ago. I want to be back in my office, fucking on my desk with you wrapped around me! I want your body underneath mine looking up at me with some expression other than the one I saw when you left me at the lifts!" I rested my forehead on the steering wheel and took in air.

"Okay . . . Ethan." Her voice sounded shaky and more than a little defeated.

"Okay, Ethan?" I mocked. "What does that mean? Okay, I'm coming home with you? Okay to you and me? Okay, I'll let you secure me? What? I need more from you, Brynne." I talked to the windshield because I was scared to see her face. What if I couldn't make her understand—

She leaned toward me and put her hand on my leg. "Ethan, I—I need—I need the truth from you. I have to know what is happening around me—"

I immediately covered her hand with mine. "I know, baby. I was wrong for keeping the information from you—"

She shook her head at me. "No, you don't know. Let me finish what I was saying." She put her fingers to my lips to shut me up. "You always interrupt me."

"Shutting up now." I grabbed at her fingers with my other hand and held them to my lips. I kissed her fingers and didn't let go. Hell, I'd take any small opportunities I could get.

"Your honesty and bluntness are two of the things I love about you, Ethan. You always told me what you wanted, what you intended to do, how you felt. You were true with me and it made me feel safe." She tilted her head and shook it. "You have no idea how much I needed that from you. I didn't fear the unknown, because you were so good at telling me exactly what you wanted to happen with us. That really worked for me. But I trusted you implicitly and you damaged that part between us by not being honest, and by not telling me you were hired to protect me. The fact I need protection at all is a mind fuck for me, but don't you think I'm entitled to fucking *know* about it?"

God, she was sexy when she was all fired up and said bad words. I gave her a moment of triumph because she was completely in the right.

When she tugged her fingers away from my lips, giving me permission to speak, I mouthed my words more than said them. "I am so sorry." And I *was* deeply sorry. I had done wrong. Brynne needed the bare-naked truth. She had her reasons; it was a requirement for her and I'd blown it. *Wait. Did she just say "the things I love about you"?*

"But . . . now that I've talked to my dad, and he's told me

things I didn't know before, I realize it's not totally your fault. Daddy put you in a position you didn't ask for . . . and I've been trying to see it from your perspective. Your letter helped me understand."

"So you forgive me and we can put this bloody mess behind us?" I was hopeful, but not completely sure. Just tell me straight up so I can guess where to go from this point. I could work with odds like that.

"Ethan, there's so much you don't know about me. You don't really know what happened to me, do you?"

Brynne gave me a look so anguished, it belied her years. I wanted to make the anguish go away if I could. I wished I could tell her it didn't matter for me to know. If it was horrible and it hurt her to tell me, then she didn't have to. But I knew this wasn't the way for Brynne. She needed to lay all her cards on the table in order to move forward.

"I guess I don't. I didn't realize your past had marked you so deeply until recently. I thought I was protecting you from possible political surveillance and exposure for harm or gain depending on who was targeting you. Once I saw that you had demons, I cared too much by that point to scare you or have you hurt by it. I only wanted to protect you and keep us together." I spoke to her face, so close to mine, soaking her molecules in with every breath.

"I know, Ethan. I get that now." She moved back fully into her seat. "But you still don't know everything." She looked away out the window again. "You won't like hearing about it. You may not . . . want . . . to be together after you know."

"Don't say that to me. I know precisely what I want." I reached for her chin and tugged her my way. "Let's get some food in you and you can tell me whatever you need to say. Yeah?"

She nodded just slightly in that acquiescent way she'd mastered—the look she was giving me made me utterly insane for her to the point where my possessiveness surprised even me.

I knew she was hurting and afraid, but I also knew she was tough and that she would fight her way through whatever haunted her. It wouldn't change how I felt, though. In my eyes, she was my beautiful American girl and she always would be.

"I'm not going anywhere, Brynne. You're stuck with me and you better get used to it," I said. I kissed her on the lips and let go of her chin.

She smiled a half smile as I put the car in reverse. "I missed you so much, Ethan."

"You have no idea." I reached out and touched her face again. I couldn't help it. Touching her meant she was really here with me. Feeling her skin and body warmth told me I wasn't dreaming it. "Food first. You are going to eat something substantial, and I'm going to watch and enjoy every second of your beautiful mouth as you do. What do you fancy right now?"

"I don't know. Pizza? I'm not exactly dressed for dinner," she smirked, gesturing to her clothes. "You have on a suit."

"How you're dressed is the least of my concerns, baby." I took her hand to my lips and kissed the soft skin. "You are beautiful to me in anything . . . or nothing. Especially nothing," I attempted teasing.

She blushed just slightly. I felt the throb in my cock when I saw her reaction. I wanted her home with me so badly. In my bed where I could reach for her all throughout the night and know she was there with me. I wasn't letting her get away again.

She once told me she loves it when I kiss her hand. And I know I cannot help myself. It's hard not to touch and kiss her all the time, because I've never been a person to deny myself much of anything I want. And I want her.

She mouthed a silent thank-you but still looked sad. She probably dreaded our conversation but knew it had to be done. For her own sake she needed to tell me something hard and I would have to listen. If this is what she needed to do in order for us to move forward, then I would hear whatever it was.

"Pizza it is, then." I had to let go of her hand to drive, but I could manage it. Just barely.

My girl was right next to me in my car. I could smell her, and see her, and even touch her if I reached out; she was that close to me. And for the first time in days, the constant ache in my chest had slipped away.

Chapter 4

♣ ♠ ♥ ♦

Candlelight and pizza are excellent with the right person. For me, the right person was sitting across from me, and it wouldn't have mattered where we were as long as we were together. But Brynne needed food and I needed to hear her story, so Bellissima's would do as well as any other place.

We had a table in a dark, private corner, a bottle of red wine, and one giant sausage-and-mushroom to share. I tried not to make her uncomfortable by staring too hard, but it was damn difficult not to because my eyes were starved for the view of her. Ravenous.

I did my best to be a considerate listener instead. Across from me Brynne looked like she was struggling with how to begin. I smiled at her and commented on how good the food tasted. I found myself wishing she would eat a little more but kept my mouth shut on that matter. I am sure I'm not a moron. I grew up with an older sister and the lessons learned from Hannah have definitely stuck with me throughout the years. Women don't like to be told about what to eat or not eat. Best to just leave her alone and hope for the best.

She looked very far away in her head when she started telling me about her life. I didn't like the sad body language or the defeated sound to her voice, but those points were irrelevant.

"My parents split when I was fourteen. I didn't handle it well, I guess. I'm an only child, so I suppose I reached out for some kind of validation or maybe it was to get back at them for the divorce. Who knows, but bottom line? I was a slut in high school." She lifted her eyes to mine, steely gray and determined to get her point across. "It's true, I was. I didn't make great choices in the boys I dated and I didn't care about my reputation. I was spoiled and immature, and very stupidly reckless."

Really! First surprise of the night. I couldn't imagine Brynne like that and didn't want to either, but the pragmatic side of me realized most everyone had a past, and my girl was no different. She picked up her wineglass and stared into it like she was remembering. I didn't say anything. I just listened and soaked in the sight of her so close to me.

"There was this news story that went viral in California a few years back. A sheriff's son made a video of a girl at a party. She was passed out drunk when he and two of his buddies fucked her and toyed with her on a pool table."

I felt the hair on the back of my neck rise up. *Please, no.*

"I remember that," I said, forcing myself to listen and trying not to react much. "The sheriff tried to suppress evidence against his son, but it leaked out and the motherfuckers got convicted anyway."

"Yeah . . . in that case they did." She looked down at her pizza and then back up at me. "Not in mine, though."

Her eyes got glassy, and suddenly I didn't feel like eating either.

"I went to a party with my friend Jessica, and we got drunk, of course. So drunk I don't remember anything that happened until I woke up and heard them laughing and talking about me." She took a big gulp of wine before she continued. "Lance Oakley was—*is*—a total asshole, an entitled, rich deviant. His dad was a California state senator at the time. I don't know why I ever went out with him. Probably because he merely asked. Like I said before, I didn't make good choices with my behavior. I took risks. That's how much I didn't care about myself."

I hate this.

"He was away at college, and I was in my senior year of high school. I guess he felt entitled whenever he came home that I would be around for him, but we weren't exclusive by any means. I know he cheated. I guess he just expected I would pine away waiting for him to come home from college and be his convenience. I did know he was mad at me for going out with another boy I met at a track meet, but not how cruel he would be because of it."

"You were track and field at your school?" I asked.

"Yeah . . . the running." She nodded and looked into her glass again. "So I wake up in a total fog, not able to move my limbs. We think he may have put something in my drinks." She swallowed hard and continued bravely on. "They were talking about me, but I didn't know it was me at first. Or what they had done to me. There were three of them, all on Thanksgiving break from college. I didn't even know the other two guys, only Lance. They were not from my school." She took a drink of her wine. "I could hear them laughing at someone. Saying how they shoved a pool stick and a bottle and—and fucked her with those things—how she was a whore who begged for it."

Brynne closed her eyes and breathed in deep. I ached for her. I wanted to kill Oakley and his friend, and wished his dead buddy was still alive so I could kill him too. I had no idea about this. I'd assumed it was just a youthful indiscretion that some idiot decided to video—not a full-blown sexual assault on a seventeen-year-old girl. I reached out for her hand and covered it with mine. She stilled for an instant and closed her eyes tighter, but she didn't flinch away. Again, her bravery humbled me and I waited for her to say more.

"I had no idea they were talking about me, though, I was so out of it. When I could move my legs and arms I struggled to get up. They laughed and left me there on the table. I knew I'd had sex, but I didn't know with whom or any details. I felt sick and hung over. I just wanted to get out of that house. So I pulled my clothes back together, found Jessica, and got a ride home."

A growl came unbidden out of my throat. I couldn't help it. Even to my ears I sounded like a dog. Brynne looked up at me almost startled for a second and then down at my hand on top of hers. I focused on her and pulled my emotions together. Losing my cool wouldn't help Brynne at all, so I brushed my thumb over her hand slowly back and forth, hoping like hell she understood how much it hurt me to hear of her being used like that. My mind was reeling with what she'd shared. At the time of the crime, the perpetrators had been adults and she'd been underage. Interesting. And I couldn't figure out why Tom Bennett had omitted this information when he'd hired me. He was likely just trying to protect the reputation of his only child. No wonder he got volatile when he found out we were sleeping together.

"I would have put the whole thing out of my mind if not for the video. I had no idea what they had done to me or that they filmed it. I came to school on a Monday and it was big news. I was big news. They'd seen me—naked, passed out drunk, being—being toyed with, fucked, used like an object—"

Tears rolled down her cheeks, but she didn't lose her composure. She kept talking and I just held on to her hand.

"Everyone knew it was me. People had watched the video all weekend and passed it around. The video showed me clearly, but the boys were off camera and the sound had been dubbed over with a song instead of audio so you couldn't hear their voices to identify them." She lowered her voice to a whisper. "Nine Inch Nails—'Closer.' They made it like a music video with the lyrics to the song printed out over the screen in big letters . . . You let me violate you—You let me penetrate you—"

She faltered, and my heart just broke in two for what she'd suffered. I knew only how much I wanted to make it work between us. I stopped her then. I had to. I couldn't listen to any more and restrain myself in public. We needed privacy for this. I just wanted to take her home with me and hold her close. The rest could be figured out later.

I squeezed her hand so she would look up at me. Big luminous eyes, in colors that all blended together, filled with glassy tears I only wanted to lick away, looked into mine. "Let me take you home, please." I nodded to make her understand it was what we needed. "I want to be alone with you right now, Brynne. Everything else doesn't matter so much."

She made a sound that just ripped my heart apart. So soft, but injured and raw. I stood up from the table abruptly, tugging her with me, and bless her heart, she followed without protesting. I threw some notes on the table and got her out to the car and buckled into her seat.

"Are you sure you want to, Ethan?" she asked me, her eyes red and full of tears.

I looked at her dead on. "I've never been surer of anything." I leaned to her and put my hand on the back of her head so I could control the kiss. I kissed her thoroughly on the lips, even pressing against her teeth with my tongue so she would open up to me. Brynne needed to know I still wanted her. I knew she was struggling with the idea of herself and my knowledge of her past. She assumed I wouldn't desire her anymore if I knew the details.

My girl could not have been more wrong.

"All of your things are still there waiting for you. Just know this . . ." I spoke directly just a few inches from her face, boring into her soulful eyes. "I have no intentions of letting you go." I swallowed hard. "If you come with me you're signing on for all of me, Brynne. I don't know any other way to be with you. It's all in for me. And I want it to be all in for you too."

"All in?" She brought her palm to my cheek and held it there, her questioning look so genuine.

I turned my lips to press them into the palm of her hand as she held my face. "A poker term. Means to bet everything you have on the cards you're holding. You're what I'm holding."

She closed her eyes again and her lip trembled slightly. "I haven't even told you all of it. There's more." She took her hand away.

"Open your eyes and look at me." I said it gently but very firmly.

She complied instantly, and I had to stifle a groan at how much her gesture aroused me. "I don't care, whatever it is you haven't told me or even what you just told me in the restaurant." I shook my head a little to make her understand. "It won't change how *I* feel. I know we'll talk some more and you can tell me the rest when you're able . . . or when you need to. I'll hear it. I need to hear everything anyway so I can make sure you're kept safe. Which I will do, I promise you, Brynne."

"Oh, Ethan—" Her bottom lip quivered as she looked over at me, as beautiful in her sadness as she was when she was happy.

I could see Brynne was worried about many things—sharing her past, my reaction to her past, the possible threats to her safety in London, my feelings—and I so desperately wanted to erase that worry from her expression if I could. I wished for her to be free from her burdens and left alone to live her life, hopefully with me in there somewhere.

I'd never meant a promise more so than right now either. I *would* keep her safe, but I also wanted to make sure she understood what she would be getting in agreeing to come home with me.

"But no more running from me, Brynne. If you need a break, that's fine, I'll respect it and give you some space. But I have to be able to come to you and see you, and know that you won't take off again . . . or shut me out." I brushed her lips with my thumb. "That's what I need from you, baby. Can you do that?"

She started breathing harder, her chest moving her breasts up and down in that tight turquoise top, her eyes flickering as she contemplated. I could tell she was scared, but Brynne had to learn to trust me if we had any chance at all together. I gambled on the hope she would take my offer. I hardly knew what to do if she didn't, though. *Fall apart? Become a real stalker? Sign up for psychotherapy?*

"But—I find it so hard to trust in a relationship. You've gotten further than anyone ever has before. For the first time I've had to choose between a complex, scary relationship and being safely uncomplicated . . . and alone."

I groaned and gripped her a little tighter. "I know you're scared, but I want you to give us a chance anyway. You're not meant to be alone. You're meant to be with me." My words came out a little hard, but it was too late to pull them back.

Brynne surprised me by smiling a little and shaking her head at me. "You're something else, Ethan Blackstone. Were you always like this?"

"Like what?"

"So demanding, blunt and direct."

I shrugged. "I guess. I don't know. I just know how I am with you. I want things with you I've not wanted before. I want you and that's all I know. Right now I want you to come home with me and be together. And I'll just take the promise that you won't leave at the first sign of trouble. You'll give me the opportunity to make it right and not close me out." I held her shoulders with both hands. "I can be understanding if you'll tell me what you need from me. I want to give you whatever it is you need, Brynne." I rubbed with my thumbs at the base of her neck, the soft skin under my fingers magnetized as soon as I began touching her. Once I got a feel of her again, I didn't want to give her up.

She tilted her head back and closed her eyes for an instant, succumbing to our attraction and giving me some hope. She said one word. My name. "Ethan."

"I think I know what that is too. You just have to trust me to give it to you." I gripped a little tighter. "Choose me. Choose us."

She shivered. I saw it happen and felt it too. She nodded and mouthed the words, "All right. I promise I won't run again."

I kissed her slowly, my hands moving up to hold her face secure. I pushed my tongue between her sweet lips, and praise the angels, she let me in. *Yes.* She allowed me passage and kissed me back, her warm, silky tongue sliding against mine. *Jackpot.* I knew I'd won this round—I wanted to slap the felt and give a silent thank-you up to my mum in heaven.

I kept plundering Brynne's mouth instead. I let her know everything in that kiss, taking her lips, grazing with my teeth, trying to get inside her. The deeper I got in, the harder it would be for her to leave me again. That's how my mind worked with her. This was battle strategy and I could do this all day. There would be no running away from me anymore, no hiding, no quarter given. She *would* be mine and let me love her.

Brynne melted under my lips, grew soft and submissive, found the place she needed and drew comfort in, just as I did in taking control. It worked for us—very, very well. I pulled back and sighed deeply. "Let's go home now."

"What happened to taking things slow?" she asked softly.

"All in, baby," I whispered, "it can't be any other way with us." If she only knew the thoughts I had for the future she might have got skittish with me again, and I couldn't risk it just yet. There would be time enough for that discussion later.

"We have a lot to talk about still," she told me.

"So we'll do a lot of talking." *Along with other things.*

She turned in her seat and leaned back, getting comfortable, and just looked at me as I pulled out of the parking lot. She watched me throughout the trip. I liked having her eyes on me. No, I fucking loved it. I loved that she was next to me looking like she wanted me as much as I wanted her. I looked at her too when I could take my eyes off the road.

"All in, huh? I think I have to learn how to play poker."

I laughed. "Oh, I'm so on board with that. Somehow I think you'll be a natural, sweetheart." I wiggled my eyebrows. "Strip poker first?"

"I was waiting for you to bring that up. Nice to know you didn't disappoint me," she said, rolling her eyes.

I just grinned and imagined her stripping in a poker game, because I would win every hand. Very, very nice imagery I conjured up too.

In the end she asked to stop by her flat so she could get her "pills." I wasn't sure if that meant birth control or the sleeping pills, and I had no intention of asking either. We definitely needed both. So I did what any bloke with a functioning brain would do. I drove her to her flat. Again, I pride myself on not being a moron.

I went upstairs and waited while she packed a bag. I told her to bring enough for a few days. What I really wanted was for her to stay at my place indefinitely, but I didn't think this was the proper moment to broach that subject—my non-moron status notwithstanding.

Memories flooded my brain when we stepped inside. The wall adjacent to the front door would forever be seared into my frontal lobe. The picture of her in that short purple dress and boots, held up by me. Christ, she'd been magnificent working out my cock up against the wall that night. *I love that fucking wall.* Funny. I smirked to myself at my clever joke.

"What are you smiling about now?" Brynne asked as she came out of her bedroom with her packed bag, looking much better than she had earlier in the evening. Her feisty personality was back.

"Ummm . . . I was just thinking about how much I love your wall." I gave her my best eyebrow quirk and took the bag from her hand.

Brynne's lovely lips parted in an expression of surprise that quickly turned to humor. "You still manage to make me laugh, Ethan, in spite of everything. You have a rare talent for it."

"Thanks. I like to share all my talents with you," I said suggestively, putting my arm around her as we came out of her flat. She glanced at the wall herself when we passed it. "I saw that," I said.

"Saw what?" she asked innocently. Oh, she had a poker face for sure. I couldn't wait to start playing cards with her.

"You looked at the wall and remembered shagging me against it."

She elbowed me playfully in the ribs as we walked. "I did no such thing! And you shagged me, not the other way around."

"Whatever." I tickled her and made her squirm into me. It felt lovely having her in my arms again. "Just fess up to the truth, baby, we had an epic shag."

By the time I got Brynne behind the closed doors of my flat, the summer night had fully settled over the city.

En route, we'd ended up stopping one final time to purchase a new mobile number and device for her. It had taken nearly an hour to get set up, but it was necessary. Her old mobile was now in my possession. Whoever rang looking for Brynne Bennett on that number would get to deal with me.

Maybe tonight I'd investigate the caller and possibly talk to Tom Bennett. Not a conversation I was thrilled about, but not one I would avoid either. *Cheers, Tom. I'm shagging your daughter again. Oh, and before I forget, you must know that her safety is completely in my hands now. Did I also mention that she is mine? Mine, Tom. I keep what's mine very close and very safe.*

I wondered how he'd take the news, and then I realized that I didn't much care. He was the one who'd put Brynne in my path. She was my priority now. I cared about her. I only wanted to protect and keep her from harm. He would have to deal with the situation just like I had to deal with it.

I walked up behind her standing at the window, staring out at the city lights. She'd told me she loved my view the first time I'd brought her home. I'd told her I loved the view of her standing in my house and that nothing compared. It still didn't in my opinion.

I touched her carefully, my hands on her shoulders, my lips at her ear. "What are you looking at?"

She saw my reflection in the glass, so she wasn't startled. "The city. I love the lights at night."

"I love looking at you looking at the lights at night." I moved her hair to the side and kissed her neck. She tilted her head to give me access as I inhaled, the scent of her skin drugging me—making me utterly mad for her. "It feels so good with you here," I whispered.

All the time I struggled with my desires when she was near. This was a new problem I'd never faced in a relationship before. I loved the shagging part—I'm a guy and I have a cock. I've never had trouble finding dates either. Women like my looks, and as Dad said, it made things easier, but not necessarily better. When women chased after you because they thought you looked hot and had a little money, it quickly reduced things down to a very basic exchange. Some dinner, some sex, maybe a second date-slash-bang-session. And then . . . good-bye. The bottom line is I don't like to be used, and I've had years of attempts from females to put me off of dating for sex.

Brynne evoked a different reaction from me, and she'd done so since the very first meeting. She never chased me, for one thing. If I hadn't heard her call me beautiful on the headset that night at the gallery, I wouldn't have known she ever saw me. She pushed all the right buttons, and for the first time I cared about the woman so much more than the sex with the woman.

Oh I still cared about the sex, but it was very different now. The dominant needs in me had blossomed since finding Brynne, as if she was the catalyst. In fact, I knew she was. I wanted things with her that frightened me because I didn't want—no, couldn't bear—to lose her over it.

What she'd shared tonight scared the absolute fucking hell out of me. It also made her mysterious behavior in the beginning very clear. I had a few answers at least about why she kept running.

"I'm glad too." She breathed out a long breath. "I missed you so much, Ethan." She leaned back into me, the curve of her bum coming right up against my hips. With just the layer of spandex from her track shorts covering that lovely part of her, my cock woke right up, ready and volunteering for duty.

Sweet Christ! That's all it took to get me started. She would feel my erection in a moment and then what? I shouldn't be coming on to her right now. She was still fragile and needed to finish her story. If only I could tell that to my cock. I turned her head to meet mine and engulfed her lips in a very deep kiss that let all the logic fall away. I nibbled and sucked on her lips, trying to pull her into me. She tasted so fine. Brynne melted right into where I wanted to take this, and I knew I wouldn't be able to pull back now. I was in very great need of claiming my woman again.

Only a bastard would want to take her to bed and get her naked right now. Ergo, I was a complete and utter dirty bastard.

I could live with that.

Brynne always told me she liked when I was blunt. She'd said she felt better about me telling her what I wanted because she knew what was coming. She needed that from me. So I took a deep breath and told her what I wanted.

"I want to take you to bed right now. I want you in my arms and I want . . . inside you." I searched her face held in my two hands and looked for her answer.

Chapter 5

♣　♠　♥　♦

want you too." She nodded and leaned up to kiss me. "Take me to bed, Ethan." The most beautiful words I'd heard in days and days met my ears. I took those sweet lips she offered and scooped her right up off the floor, her body tight against my chest.

She wrapped her legs around my hips and buried her face at my neck. I groaned out loud and started walking. When I got us to the bedroom, the sight of the bed made up with clean sheets had never been more welcome. *Monday!* Annabelle had come, thank the blessed gods! If those sheets from this morning had still been there with the evidence of my pitiful wanking session all over them, I don't know what I would have done. I made a mental note to give Annabelle a nice thank-you-for-being-discreet tip.

I laid Brynne out on her back and just looked down at her for a moment. The need to go slow was important this time. I wanted to cherish her and accept this gift she was giving to me. I needed to savor her.

Her hair swept over her shoulders and her eyes looked sort of green against the turquoise top she still wore. *Not going to be wearing it for long.*

I started on her trainers. Then the ankle socks. I cupped her feet and massaged them before sliding up her leg and hips to the waistband of her shorts. My fingers slipped underneath and gripped. Down they came. My eyes took in the reveal of her skin as the fabric slipped away—navel, hip bones, stomach, pussy, and long legs. Legs that would wrap around me when I was deep inside that beautiful, bare quim of hers. *Sweet Christ.*

There was a reason my girl was a model. *A nude model.* She possessed a body that had the power to render me speechless. I wasn't done revealing my masterpiece yet, though. I reached for her top. It was a one-stop shop too. Nothing underneath. I wanted to shout out a triumphant *YES*. Her breasts spilled out to the side as soon as I got that shirt off over her head.

"Brynne . . . beautiful." I heard the sound of her name come off my lips but couldn't remember intending to say it. I had to see her naked again, to remember how she looked, to know I had the right to touch her and that she'd accept me. I had to have some small part of her inside me before I could do anything else too, I was that desperate.

Slowly I dragged my mouth from her navel up to one perfect breast, covered the whole nipple and sucked deep. I pulled her up inside my mouth and caressed the underside with my fingers. *So soft.* She budded up tight and hard underneath my tongue, and I had to give consideration to the other one to be fair. Those beauties deserved an absolutely equal share of my attentions for sure.

She looked so yielding and sensual lying there for me to fill my eyes with her image. Like a portrait. But one that only I would ever see. *That's not true.* The nagging irritation was fleeting as I pushed the idea of others seeing her naked down deep into the dungeon of my mind. Right now I had a feast before me. It was time to partake.

I needed to feel that flesh against my tongue and lips. I needed so much from her that I was shaking as I kicked off my shoes and reached for my belt. I stripped out of my clothes fast, very aware that Brynne watched every move I made, her eyes traveling all over me. The sight of her admiring made me so hard my balls hurt and my cock burned. *Only for her.*

I lowered onto the bed with my knees leading, totally distracted about where to go first. She was a banquet for me all splayed out, her legs bent slightly but not revealing what I wanted to see. My urges rose up from somewhere and the words came out of my mouth. "Open up and show me. I want to see what's mine, baby."

Slowly, her feet slid upward until they were flat on the sheets as she bent her legs at the knees. I held my breath and felt the thud of my heart in my chest. She shifted one leg over and then the other. Just like that. She did what I'd asked of her. Perfect submission in a graceful maneuver that ran a jolt of lust up my cock just from the show she was giving me. I was nowhere near satisfied. I wanted a good long look before I started in on what I'd been denied for too many days.

"Put your hands up over your head and hold on to the bed."

Her eyes flickered a bit and focused on my mouth.

"Trust me. I'm gonna make it so good for you, baby. Let me do this my way."

"Ethan," she whispered, but she did what I asked, slowly bringing her arms up to cross wrists over her head and grip the edge of the mattress. God, I loved when she said my name during sex. I loved when she said it, period.

"Baby." Her breasts puddled to the sides and up a little with the rise of her arms. Those perfect raspberry-tipped nipples begged for more of my tongue. I went back to them, sucking and tweaking the sensitive flesh, loving how she moved beneath my mouth. She flowed in a rhythm with me.

I dragged my lips off her. My fingers reached out for a nipple and rolled it around before pulling the tip up in a little pinch. She moaned and arched for me but kept her arms up. I pinched the other one and watched her flex her hips a little, her legs widening and displaying even more of that part of her I needed to know again.

"You're so beautiful like this," I said against her stomach as I kissed my way down to the place I wanted my mouth against. I kissed first and loved her response. She trembled beneath my touch. I flicked my tongue over her folds, pressing her open like a blossom. *Mine.* She flexed her muscles and whimpered. Small, soft sounds of pleasure and need. Need for what I could give to her. Need for *me.*

"You are . . . so fucking beautiful, Brynne," I murmured against her flesh.

"You make me feel beautiful," she stuttered in a whisper and opened up a little more underneath me.

"That's it . . . give yourself over to *me,* baby." I kissed her pussy lips just like I would her mouth. "I'm going to make you come so hard, and you're going to think of nothing but me when I do," I told her.

"Please make me . . ."

I growled against her flesh. "Making you come under my tongue is the sexiest thing in the world. How you move. How you taste. How you sound when you get there . . ."

"Ahhh," she moaned and moved beneath me. *Such a gorgeous sound.* I went to work on her in earnest as she cried out, arching her hips to meet my mouth. I held her open and devoured the quivering softness. I couldn't stop and I couldn't slow down. Her quim up against my lips, where my tongue could find its way inside her over and over again, was all I cared about. I kept it up, sweeping over her clit until I felt her go off.

"Oh, God, Ethan!" she cried softly, convulsing as her climax took over.

"Uh-huh," I groaned, barely able to speak. "Now you're going to do that again!" I told her as I moved up and aligned my cock. I flinched when our parts touched, like a jolt of electricity charged me. Our eyes met and hers widened in that instant before I took her.

I buried my cock on a hard, slick thrust, unable to deny myself for another second. She moaned the sexiest sound I've ever heard when I sank down into her. Fuck, she felt good—tight and hot and swallowing me in, her inner muscles clenching around me through the force of her ongoing climax. It was something so fine it frightened me to realize the power she held over me. Brynne held me captive as she had done from the first. Sex was no different. She held me captive all of the time.

She moved with me, accepting every stroke like she needed it from me to live.

"I'm going to fuck you until you come again!"

And I did.

Brynne took it all; every pounding drive of my cock into her sweet cove, the sound of our bodies slapping together filling the air, bringing us closer to the end. I loomed over her face with mine, gripping her eyes with mine, owning her body with mine. I saw only her. I felt only her. I heard only her.

She tensed deep inside and rolled her eyes back, her mouth falling open. I took that too. I covered her lips with mine and thrust inside with my tongue. I swallowed her cries when she started to orgasm and gave her mine when the rush hit me in the balls. This was going to be immense: a blast of something indescribable, pleasure that belied words to express what it felt like, shot up my cock. I could only get lost in her and ride it out as I fell into oblivion with the explosion.

My body slowed to a stop and just stayed buried inside her, still convulsing through the pulses. I didn't want to ever leave where I was. How could I?

Time stilled and we breathed. The simplest task of taking in oxygen was all-consuming. I could feel her heart pounding beneath my chest and the little spasms of pleasure being drawn out to the last around my cock from the tight walls of her quim. *So fucking good.*

When I could bear to pull my mouth away from her skin, I hovered over her face, searching her eyes for something good. I was afraid of what I might see. The last time we'd been like this together, very bad things happened in the next moments. *She told you to get off her and walked out the door.*

"I do love you." I whispered the words, barely audible just inches away from her face, and watched her eyes grow luminous and then wet. She started to cry.

Not really the reaction I'd hoped for. I pulled out of her body and felt the gush of wet between us. But Brynne surprised me yet again. Instead of distancing herself, she burrowed right up against my chest, held on to me and sobbed quietly. She wept but wasn't trying to get away from me. She was seeking comfort. I realized I would never understand a woman's mind.

"Tell me everything will be okay . . . even if it won't," she said between sobs.

"It will be, baby. I'll make sure." I wanted a Djarum so bad I could taste it. Instead I held her against me and stroked over her hair, twining my fingers through its silkiness over and over again until she stopped crying.

"Why?" she asked after a while.

"Why what?" I kissed her forehead.

"Why do you love me?" Her voice was low but the question very clearly heard.

"I can't change how I feel or know *why*, Brynne. I just know you're my girl and I've had to follow my heart." She still couldn't tell me the same. I knew she cared for me, but I think she was more convinced that she was undeserving of love more than anything. Either giving or receiving.

"I haven't told you the rest of the story yet, Ethan."

Bingo. "What are you afraid of?" I asked. She stiffened in my arms. "Tell me what frightens you, baby."

"That you'll stop."

"Stop loving you? No. I won't."

"But when you know everything? I'm a mess, Ethan." She looked up at me with her eyes sparking different colors again.

"Hmmm." I kissed the end of her nose. "I know enough already, and it changes nothing about how I feel. You can't be any worse than me. I command you to stop worrying. And you're right. You are a mess down here, and I made you that way." I snaked my hand down between her legs and slid my fingers all along the center of her and felt what I'd put there. The caveman in me loved the idea of all that spunk I'd put inside her, but she probably didn't. "Take a bath with me and we can talk some more."

Her eyes widened from my touch but she nodded her head and said, "That sounds nice."

I rolled off the bed and went in to start the bathwater. Her eyes tracked me, looking over my back. I knew she was staring at the scars. I knew she'd ask me about them soon too. And I would have to share my fucked-up train wreck of a past. I didn't want to. The thought of bringing her into that clusterfuck went against every instinct I possessed, but still, I wouldn't ever keep the truth from her again. That wasn't an option with Brynne, and I'd learned my lesson.

I poured in some bath bubbles and adjusted the temperature. I looked up at the sight of her walking into the bathroom. Naked and beautiful and coming toward me, she took my breath away even if she'd gotten too slim. I found myself thinking about another round of prehistoric shagging but forced it down so the rational part of my brain could function. We really needed to talk through some things, and sex had a way of pushing to the front of the queue and overshadowing everything else. *The greedy, lecherous bastard.*

So I took her hand instead and helped her step into the tub with me and got us settled. I sat down and put her in front of me, her slippery bum resting temptingly against my suddenly reawakening cock. I told my tackle to shut the hell up, and to imagine Muriel the street vendor and her accompanying mustache if he wanted more of Brynne's divine fanny. That did the trick. Muriel was hideous, and probably not even a real woman. Maybe not even human. In fact, I'm sure Muriel is really an alien scout sent here to sell newspapers and learn the language. I still craved my Djarums. Piles of them.

Brynne sniffed the air. "Do you smoke in here?"

"Sometimes." *I really need to stop doing that.* "But I'll have to stop it inside the house now that you're here with me."

"I don't mind it, Ethan. The smell of the spice and the cloves is nice and it doesn't bother me, but I know it's bad for you and I don't like that part."

"I'm trying to quit." I slid my hands up her arm and then down over a breast resting just at water level. "With you here I'll do better. You can be my motivation, okay?"

She took a deep breath and nodded. Then she started talking.

"I never went back to my high school again. Only six months from graduation and I quit. My parents were in shock at the change in me. It didn't take long for them to find out about the video either. They argued about what to do, and had very differing opinions. I didn't care. I was someplace else in my head and very, very sick. It's hard to admit about myself, but it's the truth. I was destroyed emotionally with no way to escape the demons."

I kissed the back of her head and held on to her a little tighter. I knew all about demons, the evil cocksuckers that they were. "Can I ask why your parents didn't try to press assault charges on the three of them? I can't imagine it would have been difficult to get an arrest. You were underage and they were adults . . . and there was videotaped evidence."

"My dad wanted them in prison. My mom didn't want the publicity. She asserted that my slutty reputation would only drag our name through the mud and upset the social order of things. She was probably right. But again, I didn't care what anyone did about it. I was lost in my head."

"Oh, baby."

"And then I discovered they'd gotten me pregnant."

I stilled at that unwelcome news. *Fucking hell* . . .

"It put me over the edge. I—I couldn't deal with any of it. My dad didn't know what to do about a pregnancy. He started talking to the senator. My mom scheduled an abortion for me, and I simply could not handle any more. I didn't want a baby. I didn't want to kill what was inside of me either. I just didn't want to be reminded of the incident and everything and everybody reminded me. I guess if I'd felt better about myself I could have figured things out, but then if I'd felt better about myself I would have never gone to that party in the first place and ended up on that pool table."

"I am so sorry." I spoke softly but firmly, wanting her to really understand how I truly felt. "Listen, baby, you cannot blame yourself for what happened to you." I pressed in close to her ear. "You were the victim of a crime and treated abominably. It was not your fault, Brynne. I hope you know that now." I rubbed up and down her arms, drawing the warm water up over her skin.

She settled more into my body and took a deep breath. "I think I do now, for the most part at least. Dr. Roswell helped me, and finding my place in the world helped too. But back then I was done. Done with living. I couldn't see another path for me."

All the warmth of earlier left me and I braced for what was coming. Like a train wreck you can't stop staring at, I had to know what had happened to her but also didn't want to know. I didn't want to go to her dark place with her.

She shifted in the bath and twirled her fingers in the water as she started speaking again. "I'd never felt so calm as I did on that day. I got up and knew what I would do. I waited until Daddy went to work. I felt bad for doing it at his house but knew that my mom would never forgive me for doing it at hers. I wrote them good-bye letters and set them out on my bed. Then I took a handful of sleeping pills

I'd stolen from my mom's stash, got in the bathtub, and cut my wrist open."

"No." My heart compressed in a painful grip, and all I could do was hold on to her, feel her warm body, and be grateful she was with me now. Imagining her at the point of taking her life, at such a young age, and feeling she had no other options was very sobering. I knew how I felt about Brynne, but this scared the shit out of me.

"But I sucked at that too. I got sleepy and didn't really cut deep enough to bleed out, or so I was told later. The pills I took were the far worse danger. Daddy found me in time. He came home for lunch to check on me. He said a weird vibe was shadowing him the whole morning and he just came home. He saved me." Brynne shuddered slightly and turned her head a little more to rest her cheek on my chest.

Thank you, Tom Bennett. "I'm so glad you sucked at it," I whispered. "My girl can't be brill at everything." I tried to lighten the mood a little, but this was not a conversation for steering. My role was to listen, so I kissed her hair again and put my hand over her heart. "When I speak to your father I'm going to thank him," I whispered.

"I woke up in a psychiatric hospital. My mother's first words were that I'd had a miscarriage and had done something very stupid and selfish, and that the doctors had to put me on a suicide watch. She didn't handle things well. I know I embarrassed her. And now that I'm older I can only imagine what I put my parents through, but she didn't seem to want to face what I had done either. Mom went on and on about what a blessing it was to have the pregnancy out of the way, like this was her biggest concern. Our relationship is not easy. She disapproves of most everything I do."

Brynne sighed again into my chest. I just kept touching her to reassure myself she was indeed here. My girl was telling me her deepest secrets, in a hot bath, naked in my arms after some really mind-blowing shagging. I didn't have any complaints. Well, maybe a few, but I wouldn't voice them to Brynne. I continued pulling warm water over her arms and breasts, and thought about how much I didn't approve of her mum. What mother would say such a thing to her daughter after a suicide attempt?

"When it was all over my parents sent me to a nice place in the New Mexico desert. It took time, but I got better and eventually learned how to deal with my past. Not faultlessly, but I managed to make some decent progress, I suppose. I discovered my interest in art and grew up."

Brynne paused again in her story, almost like she was gauging how I was accepting her news and if I was shocked or horrified by her now. She worried far too much. I picked up her wrist with the scars and kissed right over the jagged marks. Little slices of white marring the otherwise perfect skin with its translucent sheen, the blue of her veins showing from underneath. The idea of her cutting into that skin made me very sad for what she had borne.

I had a sudden epiphany—Brynne had made her attempt at around the same time I was in that Afghan prison about to be—

She entwined her fingers with mine and drew me out of my thoughts, bringing our hands right up to her mouth and holding them there with her lips. Brynne was kissing *my* hand this time. I felt warmth flush all throughout my body and tried to hold on to the wonderfulness of the sensation while it lasted, because her gesture made me far too emotional to speak.

"I never knew that my dad went to Senator Oakley and basically blackmailed him. He was livid that he'd nearly lost me and blamed Lance Oakley for everything. My dad wanted to press charges but realized I was in no shape to withstand a trial and probably never would be. And the added bonus of my mother telling him to leave it alone and allow me to heal in peace convinced him to let the idea of a formal prosecution go. But Daddy still wanted retribution of some form. Senator Oakley just wanted all the ugly to go far, far away from his political career, so he forced his son to enlist in the army and solved his biggest problem when Lance was shipped off to Iraq. Then he arranged for my acceptance at the University of London when the time came that I was well enough to leave New Mexico and go off to college. We decided on London mostly because it was so far away from home and the art was here. I could speak the language and Aunt Marie lived here already, so I wouldn't be completely on my own in a foreign country without at least *some* family."

"So the senator has known exactly where you were all these years?" The situation sucked, was much bigger than I ever imagined, and the risks to Brynne could be enormous.

"I never knew that part until last week," she whispered. "I thought I got in on my own merits."

"I can understand how that might bother you, but your graduate study was earned on your merits as exemplary in your field. I've seen you at work, and I know you're brilliant at what you do." I teased with my tone and kissed the side of her jaw. "My adorable anorak, Professor Bennett."

"Anorak?" she laughed. "What kind of crazy Brit slang word is that?"

"Yeah, I think you Yanks call them nerds or geeks. That's you. An artsy anorak that I adore." I turned her head to mine and met her lips for another kiss. I knew we were both remembering our ridiculous chat in the car that morning about the professor detaining the misbehaving student. Which would be her, the professor, and me, the misbehaving student.

"You're crazy," she said against my lips.

"Crazy for you," I said, squeezing her a little. "But really, Senator Oakley owed you a hell of a lot more than what he gave, although it doesn't make me happy to know that he is very aware of exactly where you are in the world and what you're doing every day."

"I know. And it scares me a little. Daddy said that Eric Montrose died in a weird bar fight when Lance was home on leave from the army. He—he was one of them . . . on the video, but I never saw any of them again after that night. Not even Lance Oakley."

The sound of her voice bothered me, and so did the thought of her remembering what she'd gone through at the hands of those degenerates. I was really happy one of them was dead. That part didn't bother me at all. I just prayed his death had nothing to do with that video and Senator Oakley's vetting.

I set the water to drain and helped her out of the tub. "I won't let anything happen to you, and you don't have to be scared. I've got it covered." I smiled and started drying her legs with a towel. "I'm going to speak to your dad tomorrow and find out everything I can on Senator Oakley." I dried her arms and back and breasts, thinking I could get really used to doing this. "You just let me worry about the senator. I'll send some feelers out and see what I get back in the way of information. Nobody's going to get near my girl unless they come through me first."

She smiled and gave me a very nice nibbling kiss on my bottom lip. I had trouble restraining myself from spreading her up on the sink counter and having her again.

Brynne's skin had a natural golden glow, but right now it was pinked from the hot water, and so beautiful it was hard to look at and stay neutral. *Don't think about it.* I ignored the urge and worked at drying her luscious curves, which had definitely lost some of their curviness but were still lovely and all *mine.* She stood gracefully for me as if not at all affected by our nakedness in such proximity. I wondered how in the hell she managed to do it. Well, I had an idea of how. She was a model who posed in the nude and she was used to it. *Don't think about that either.*

I couldn't remember ever being driven by my cock in the way I was driven with her. Maybe when I was just starting out, but nothing with this level of intensity had ever consumed me like it did now. Fucking Brynne was right up there with food and shelter these days.

Everyone needs the basics, Brynne. Food, water . . . a bed.

She provoked emotions in me I didn't know existed until the night she strolled into the Andersen Gallery talking bollocks about me and my trusty hand.

She tugged the towel away from me with a sexy smirk and used it to wrap up all that glorious nakedness in fluffy cream cotton. *A damn shame*. She walked into the bedroom and I could hear drawers opening and closing. I loved the sounds of her in there, moving around and preparing for bed. I pulled a towel down for myself and started drying off, immensely grateful I would sleep with her in my arms tonight.

Chapter 6

♣ ♠ ♥ ♦

I opened my eyes in the dark to the scent of Brynne up my nose and smiled when I figured out where we were. *She's in your bed with you.* I was careful to be still so as not to disturb her sleeping. She faced me, but her head was turned down and curled around her arm. Entranced and content for the first time in days, I just watched her breathe for a few minutes. I wanted to touch my girl, but I let her sleep. By God she needed it.

Need. So much need inside me now. Needs only Brynne could satisfy, and that scared me. I couldn't imagine feeling this way about any woman just a month ago, and now I couldn't imagine not having her in my life. The time apart had changed me forever, I feared.

I inhaled deeply and held it. The faint smell of sex was in the sheets from earlier, but mostly it was just her clean, flowery scent that intoxicated me. It intoxicated me now just as it had intoxicated me on the very first night we met. She smelled so good I hated to leave her alone in the bed, but I got up carefully and threw on some joggers and a T-shirt.

I headed across the great room and down the hall to my office, leaving the bedroom door open a crack in case Brynne woke with a bad dream. I really needed a smoke, and I really needed to talk to her dad.

"Tom Bennett." His clipped American accent on the other end of my mobile reminded me of how far away Brynne was from her family, although I must admit I loved that she considered London her home now.

"It's Ethan." I dragged in a deep inhale off my cig.

A beat of silence and then rushed questions. "Is Brynne safe? What's happened? Where is she?"

"Nothing's happened, Tom. She's sleeping right now and perfectly safe." I inhaled again.

"You're with her? Wait. Is she at your place right now?" The silence grew very thick and questioning as Tom Bennett contemplated exactly what I'd been doing with his daughter. "So you two have worked it out. Look, I'm sorry about that call I made—"

"You're sorry?" I interrupted him. "And yes, Brynne is with me at the moment and I plan to keep her *very* close, Tom." I stubbed out my Djarum and decided against lighting up a new one until after this conversation was done. "Just so you know, I'm not going to apologize for being with her either. You set this whole thing up. I'm just the simple bloke who fell for a beautiful, lovely girl. Can't help that now, can we?"

Tom made a noise that sounded like frustration to me. I had to give him credit for not exploding, but maybe he still had it in him. "Look, Ethan . . . I only want her safe. Brynne makes her own decisions in regards to who she wants to date. I just want those bastards to keep away from her. From reminding her of all the bad shit. You have no idea how she's suffered. It nearly destroyed her."

"I know. She told me *everything* tonight. I have a few things to say to you as well."

"Go ahead," Tom said impatiently.

"First, I want to thank you for acting on your ominous vibe and coming home for lunch to check on her that day. And second, I want to ask you something." I paused for effect. "What in the motherfuck were you thinking by not telling me what really happened to your daughter? Knowledge is power, Tom. How in the hell can I keep her protected when I don't know what they did to her? What Brynne described to me was not some indiscreet sex tape, as you alluded to; it was a criminal act of assault and abuse upon a seventeen-year-old girl by three legally adult men."

"I know that," he said in a defeated voice. "I didn't want to break her trust and disclose the details to you or anyone. That story is hers and hers alone to tell."

Fuck this. I lit up a second. "You left out the part about the senator getting her the scholarship to University of London. He knows exactly where she is, and has for years."

"I realize that, and again, I only wanted to get her as far away from those people as possible!" he gritted back. "I know this situation is potentially a disaster and leaves my daughter in the worst sort of position! Now do you see why I need you? This whole thing would have slipped away into oblivion if not for that plane crash. Who would have imagined Oakley being vetted as the next vice president!"

I sighed loudly. "I'm working on him, and so far I'm not finding any dirtiness popping up about the senator. I know his boy is trouble, but Senator Oakley's black book is neat and tidy."

"Well, I don't trust him. And now one of those fucking degenerates is out of the picture! This story is everything the senator wishes dead and buried, and right now, my daughter is in the middle of that shit pile! This is unacceptable!"

"You're right, and I'm watching them all, believe me. I have some contacts in the SF that are looking into the son's military record. If there's anything there, I'll find it. Question for you: Brynne said the only person identifiable on the video was herself? She told me the others were mostly off camera and their voices dubbed over with a song—"

"I—I saw it. I saw what they did to my baby girl." The man sounded broken now.

I closed my eyes and willed the images to just fade away. I couldn't imagine being in his shoes, having seen that vileness and not trying to kill who hurt her. Tom Bennett got praise for not becoming a murderer in my book.

I cleared my throat so I could speak. "There's something else you need to know about me."

"What's that?"

"She's my responsibility now. I call the shots, and I make the contact with Oakley's people when and if the time comes.

Brynne is an adult and we are together. And if you're worried about my motives for telling you this, don't be. I love her, Tom. I'm going to do whatever it takes to keep her safe and happy." I took a final drag on the smoke and let my words sink in.

He sighed before he answered. "I have two things to say to that. From a client who needs you, I wholeheartedly agree. I know you're the man for the job. If anyone can see Brynne through this mess, it will be you."

He paused, and I could guess what was coming next.

"But as a father who loves his daughter—and you really cannot understand until it happens to you—if you hurt her in this and break her heart, I am coming after you, Blackstone, and I'll have forgotten we were ever friends."

I grinned in my chair, glad that this conversation was out of the way. "Fair enough, Tom Bennett. I can live with those terms."

We spoke a bit more and I got the full backstory on the Oakleys of San Francisco. I arranged for us to talk again soon, to keep him abreast of any new developments, and ended the call.

I stayed at my desk for a bit, wrote up some notes, and sent some emails before shutting down my laptop. As I turned out the light, Simba fluttered madly in the aquarium glowing behind my desk. I went back and tossed him a treat before heading out to the balcony to sit for a while.

I passed the bedroom and heard nothing but silence. I wanted Brynne to sleep well. No more nightmares for my girl. She'd been through enough for a lifetime already.

The night sky held millions of stars tonight. It wasn't often they were so sparkly, and I realized it'd been a long time since

I had sat out here. I lit up another clove. This one was a throw-away, though. If I smoked outside, then nobody had to know about it. I shouldn't smoke inside with Brynne here anyway.

I crossed my feet up on the ottoman and leaned back into the lounger. I let my mind wander into thoughts of today and all that had happened. I thought about Brynne's tragic story and just how things had altered now. For both of us. Yeah . . . our times of darkness had been like a parallel universe. She'd been seventeen and I'd been twenty-five. Both of us in a very bad place. I felt more connected to her than ever, sitting out here alone, dragging spiced tobacco into my lungs.

I used to smoke Dunhills. It was my brand of choice and top of the line. I like fine things, so they were no surprise. But that all changed after Afghanistan. Lots of things changed after that place. I absorbed the nicotine my body craved and looked up at the myriad of stars shining overhead.

. . . Every guard smoked clove tobacco. Every last moth-erfucking rebel had one of those lovely, imperfect handrolleds hanging off his lips as they went about their tasks of beatings and mind fucks. And the smell? Like pure ambrosia. I dreamed in smokes in the first days of my capture. I dreamed about the sweet scent of clove mixed with tobacco until I was sure I would die before I ever tasted one. The beatings and interrogations started later. I don't think they knew what they had captured at first. All in good time, though, and they did figure it out even-tually. The Afghans wanted to use me to negotiate the release of their own. I got that much from their nearly insensible rant-ing. Was totally out of my hands, though. Government policy is no negotiation with terrorists, so I knew they would be disap-pointed. And I knew they would take out their frustrations on

me. Which they did. I often wondered if they knew how close I'd come to breaking in the beginning. I had terrible guilt for knowing the truth, and felt great relief I'd never had to choose, but there were some interrogations (if you could call them such) where I would have sung like a canary in a coal mine if they'd offered me one of those beautiful, sweet, clove handrolleds to smoke. It was the very first thing I asked for when I walked out of that rubble pile. The U.S. Marine who got to me first said I was in shock. I was ... and I wasn't, I suppose. I think he was in shock that anyone came out of what was left of my prison alive after they bombed it to shit (which I thanked him nicely for). But really I was in shock because I knew in that instant that the fates had changed for me. I had finally found some luck. Or luck had finally found me. Ethan Blackstone was a lucky, lucky man—

A shadow moved the faint light behind me and caught my attention. I turned my head. My heart lurched inside my chest to see Brynne standing just on the other side of the sliding glass, watching me. We stared at each other for a beat or two until she slid open the door and stepped out.

"You're up," I said.

"You're out here smoking," she said.

I set my cig in the ashtray and held my arms open to her. "You caught me."

She came right over, looking decadently tousled from sleep in a light blue T-shirt and a pair of my silk boxers. *And nothing underneath them.* I tugged her down to me and she smiled a little, folding her long legs on either side of mine, straddling my lap and holding my face in her two hands.

"You are so busted, Blackstone." Her eyes moved infinitesimally, trying to read me. I knew that's what she was doing, and I so wished I could know what she was really thinking. Just the fact that she had crawled up on my lap and held my face thrilled me, but seeing her relaxed and happy after waking in the night pleased me more.

"Mmmmm, I know how you can punish me if you want," I told her.

She snuggled against me and I drew my arms around her. "What were you thinking about? You looked very far away, sneaking your cigarette out here in the dark."

I spoke into her hair and moved my hand up and down her back. "I was thinking about . . . luck. Being lucky. Having some." It was the truth and the reason I still breathed even if I couldn't share that part with her yet. I wanted to, but didn't know how to even begin that journey with Brynne. She didn't need more painful shit piled on top of what she already had to carry around.

"And are you? Lucky?"

"I didn't used to be. But then my luck changed for the better one day. I took the gift handed me and started playing cards."

She traced over my chest with her fingers very softly, probably unaware of how much she got to me.

"You won a lot of tournaments. My dad told me that's how he met you."

I nodded against her head, my lips still on her hair. "I liked your dad very much when we first met. I still do. I talked to him tonight."

Her hand on my chest stilled for a moment but then resumed the soft rubbing. "And how did that go?"

"It went just about like I imagined it would. We both

said what we needed to say and got down to brass tacks. He knows about us. I told him. He wants the same as me—to keep you safe and happy."

"I do feel safe with you . . . I always have. And I know my dad respects you very much. He told me how he had to push you to take me on." She made a sound against me, her mouth right over my pectoral. A nice sound; soft and pretty, and one that got me very hard. "I just wish he had told me what was happening with you." She paused and then whispered longingly, "I have to know what's going on, Ethan. I can't ever go back to being the unaware victim. Secrets will destroy me—I just can't handle them now. I'll always have to know everything. Waking up like that and finding myself on that table, not knowing who or what—I can't—"

"Shhhhh, I know." I stopped her before she could get too worked up. "I realize that now."

I reached for her face. I wanted to see her eyes when I told her the next part. She was absolutely beautiful looking up at me in the starry nighttime light from where she rested on my chest. Her lips needed kissing and I wanted to be inside her again, but I forced myself to speak instead. "I am so sorry for keeping secrets. I understand why you need transparency. I get it, and I promise to tell you everything from now on, even if I think you won't like to hear it. And I know that was hard for you to tell me your story tonight, but I want you to know I am so damn proud of you. You are so strong and lovely and brilliant, Brynne Bennett. My beautiful American girl." I rubbed over her lips with my thumb.

She smiled with half of her mouth up at me. "Thank you," she mouthed.

"And you know what the best part is?" I asked.

"Tell me."

"You're here with me. Right here, where I can do this." I dipped my hand up under her shirt and cupped a breast, so soft, filling my hand with its gentle weight. I smiled at her. The kind of smile I can feel on my face, and pretty much only give to her and a very short list of others.

"I am," she said. "And I'm glad I'm here with you, Ethan. You're the first person to make me . . . forget." Her voice grew softer but, strangely, more clear. "I don't know why it works with you, but it does. I—I couldn't do—intimacy for a long time. And then it was still difficult those times I tried—"

"It doesn't matter anymore, baby," I interrupted. I hated to even imagine Brynne with someone else; another man seeing her naked, touching her, making her come. The images drove me mad with jealousy, but what she'd just told me also made me so damn happy at the same time. I was the first person to make her forget. *Fuck yes!* And I'd make it so I'd be the last person she'd ever remember too.

"I have you now, and I'm holding on to you, and I don't ever want to let you go."

She purred at me and her eyes flared as I palmed her other breast and found her tight-budded nipple. She had sensitive nipples and I loved to devour them. And make her want me. This was the real motivation, if I was honest. Making Brynne want *me* was my obsession.

I moved her hair aside and latched onto her neck with my lips. I loved the taste of her skin and how she responded when I touched her. We had chemistry together, and I knew this from the very beginning. Right now she was arching into my chest, bumping her breast further into my hand. I pinched the nipple and relished the sound she made when I did that. I knew where this was leading, or where I wanted it to lead. *Me moving inside her, making her come, her getting that soft, gorgeous look in her eyes after she climaxed.* I lived for that look in her eyes. That look drove me into behaviors I had never even considered before with a woman.

She started to grind on my lap. Her hips rocked over my now very aroused cock under the thin fabric of the joggers, making me envision all sorts of kinky things I could try. And man, did I want to try out some kink with her.

I snaked my hand up through the leg of the silk boxers she had on and right to her cleft. *Easy access.* And so fucking wet for me I could only forge ahead for more. She made sounds when I touched her quim and started circling over her tight bud of a clit that wanted my cock knocking against it. She wanted me. I made her want me sexually. If it was the best I could do with her for now, then I would take what I could get. I wanted more from my Brynne, though. So much more.

I dragged my mouth away from her neck and my hand from her pussy and lifted her off my lap to stand before me. I stayed in the lounger and flicked my gaze over her. "Strip for me."

She wobbled on her feet a bit, looking down at me, her expression unreadable. I didn't know what she would do with the command, but I didn't care. I was about to find out, and the thrill of the challenge hardened me to iron.

"But we're outside . . ." She turned to look off the balcony and then back to me.

"Get naked and climb back on top of me."

She started breathing heavier, and I still wasn't sure what she would do, but I told her anyway. Brynne liked it when I was blunt.

"No one can see. I want to fuck right here, right now, under the stars," I said.

She stared me down with those eyes of hers whose color cannot be named and brought her hands to the bottom of her T-shirt. She swept it up and off in a blink, but held it in one hand for a moment before releasing the fabric and letting it drop to the balcony floor. That delay, that look she gave me was pure unadulterated sexy. My girl knew how to play this game. She also had the most gorgeous tits in the world.

She moved to the waistband of the shorts next. Her thumbs dug in under the elastic. My mouth began to water as they started down. She bent gracefully and stepped out of my silk boxers. She stood utterly bare for me, legs slightly parted, her hair wildly mussed from sleep, waiting for me to say what to do next.

"God, just look at you. There's nothing you could tell me that would change how I feel about you or make me want you less." My cock pounded with its own heartbeat, dying to spunk her up. "Believe me," I told her, my tone carrying a bit of a sting.

She got a look on her face that suggested my words relieved her. Brynne still had so much doubt in her about how her past might change my feelings for her. *I have to work on showing her that it's inconsequential to me.* "Come here, beautiful."

She came to me and crawled onto my lap again, folding her legs and settling right over my cock with only a layer of soft cotton separating our skin. I went for her tits first, cupping one in each hand and squeezing. They filled my hands exactly, not overflowing but a soft weight that tantalized with the promise of claiming another part of her body for my own. *Perfection.*

She arched back when I bit over a nipple. Not hard, but enough to give her a little twinge and then a glorious moan when I soothed it with my tongue. I wondered how she'd do with clamps. I bet I could get her to orgasm. In fact, I pretty much knew I could. She would be something magnificent to watch when it happened. I worked over the other breast and felt her stiffen, curling back in my arms, all splayed out and warm . . . and gorgeous.

I had to be inside her. To feel Brynne orgasm around my fingers or tongue or cock was an indescribable sensation, one I had become addicted to. I moved my hand down her back, sliding over her bum in a trail, going further down and underneath to meet her wet slit from behind. She gasped a soft sound when my fingers touched her quim, and she moaned when they penetrated her wet heat in a deep grip.

"You're mine," I told her in a whisper, just inches from her face. "This pussy is mine. All the time. Whether it's my fingers or my tongue or my cock."

She flared her eyes at me as my fingers went to work. I took her mouth and buried my tongue as far as I could in tandem with what my fingers were doing between her thighs. Those gorgeous thighs spread open over my lap because I'd told her to do it.

I was so sexed out I'm sure I was too rough with her, but I couldn't seem to rein it in. She didn't protest, and if she had, I would've stopped. Every response, every sound and sigh, every undulation over my cock, told me that, in fact, she got off on it. Brynne liked me dominant when we fucked, and I loved her exactly how she was with me.

Holding her this way, with my arm down behind her hips, forcing her ever closer against me, was something I had to do. I wanted her to understand that I couldn't let her go again. I wouldn't let her go.

I guess it was the need inside me to possess her. I'd needed the control during sex before, but not like this. Brynne did something to me I couldn't even comprehend. Never before had I felt this way. *Only with her.*

I tugged her weight up off my hips. She got the idea and held herself suspended, enough for me to let go and to shove down the waist of my joggers. Not the easiest of tricks, but required if I wanted to be in her, and she seemed so on board with my plan. I held my cock straight up and told her on a harsh breath, "Right here. And fuck me good."

I think I might have actually got a tear or two in my eyes when she slid down on me and started to move. I know I wanted to. I felt my eyes water at the first touch of her cunt surrounding my cock with all that slippery, lush heat, and during the wild ride as she bucked up and down, shagging me into oblivion. And then again when I blew my load inside her. I managed to pull another orgasm from her with my thumb rubbing her sweet spot, and cherished every whimper and sound she made as she reached her peak a moment later. She came hard all around me. My name on her lips as it happened was the best, though. *Ethan . . .*

When she collapsed on top of me, my cock was still in spasms, buried inside her deep, rocked by the convulsions as her inner muscles grabbed and pulled. I was certain I could stay inside her forever.

I held us together, never wanting to separate our bodies. We stayed out on the deck for a while. I just held her to me and rubbed up and down her spine with my fingertips. She nuzzled against my neck and chest, and felt very soft and warm despite it being night, and we were outside, and she was totally naked. I pulled the throw blanket off the other lounger and drew it around her.

For the first time I understood what people meant when they said they cried because they were so happy.

Chapter 7

♣ ♠ ♥ ♦

Go ahead and pick out the one you like for today," I told her. Brynne grinned from my wardrobe door and then disappeared back into it.

"Well, I love the purple ones, but I think today we'll go with this one," she announced as she emerged with a blue tie in her hand. She sauntered up to me and draped the silk around my neck. "It matches your eyes, and I love the color of your eyes."

I love when you say the word love *in reference to anything about me.*

I watched her expression as she worked on knotting my tie, biting just the corner of her luscious bottom lip in concentration; I was loving her attentions and not loving the fact that she had obviously practiced on somebody else. She had stood right up against some other bloke and tied his tie for him. I knew it. I tried not to envision that it was morning when she performed this service for the cocksucker and that she'd not spent the previous night sucking said cocksucker's cock. I was such a jealous bastard now. I'd never been jealous with any of the girls I'd dated before, but then again, Brynne was not just a girl to me. Brynne was *the* girl. *My* girl.

"I love that you're here doing this for me," I told her.

"I am too." She smiled up at me for an instant before returning to the task at hand.

There was so much more I wanted to say but didn't. Pushing her never worked out, and I'd learned my lesson in that regard, but still it was hard to take things slow. I didn't want slow with Brynne. I wanted fast and intense and all the time. *Thank Christ I didn't say that aloud.*

"What's your day look like, Miss Bennett?" I asked instead.

"I'm having a lunch meeting with colleagues from the university. Keep your fingers crossed for me. I have to start thinking about getting that work visa, and there could be something in this for me. Like a conservancy appointment at a major London museum." She finished my tie and patted it. "There. You look very spiffy in your blue tie, Mr. Blackstone." She held her lips up to mine with her eyes closed.

I kissed her with just the tiniest peck on her puckered lips. She opened her eyes and narrowed them, looking a tad disappointed. "Expecting something more, were you?" I loved teasing her and making her laugh.

She fronted like she didn't care. "Meh," she said with a shrug. "Your kisses are . . . passable, I suppose. I can do without."

I laughed at the expression on her face and tickled her in the side. "It's a good thing you conserve paintings, my darling, because you can't lie worth shit."

She shrieked at the tickling and tried to get away.

I snaked my arms around her and hauled her against me. "No escape for you," I muttered against her lips.

"What if I don't want to escape?" she asked against mine.

"That works too," I answered with a real kiss. I went slow and thorough, enjoying this early morning moment together before we had to go to our jobs. She melted into me so sweetly that I had to remember we both had work and there was no time to take her back to bed now. The nice part was that we would be here at the end of the day again, and I could make good on my very vivid imagination.

I got to kiss her good-bye a few more times before we went our separate ways: waiting at the lifts, in the parking garage up against the Rover, and when I dropped her off at the Rothvale. Such are the benefits of having somebody you want to be with so madly in your life. Again, I am a lucky, lucky man. At least I am smart enough to realize it.

I went through the front entrance today after parking because I wanted to buy every major U.S. newspaper and have them scoured for any small thing. They'd be crammed with political mudslinging by now, but the full-bore fight between candidates was a ways off yet. Presidential elections were held the beginning of November in the U.S., so there were five months more of publicity. I felt a pang of worry and pretty much ignored it. I could not fail in protecting her. I wouldn't allow a failure.

Muriel grinned at me when I paid for the papers. I tried not to shudder at the sight of her teeth. "There you go, luv," she said, holding out a stained hand with my change.

I got a look at that grimy hand and decided she needed the change more than I needed to contract a contagion. "Keep it." I looked into her oddly beautiful green eyes and nodded once. "I'll be getting all these U.S. papers regular from now on if you want to have them ready," I offered.

"Oh, you're a darling, you are. I'll have 'em. G'day to ye, handsome." She winked at me and showed a bit more of those horrifying teeth. I tried not to look too close, but I think Muriel could compete with me on beard stubble. Poor thing.

When I got into my office I started on the intel in earnest. I listened to the message of the man who'd called Brynne. I played it several times. American, very matter-of-fact, non-confrontational, nothing in his inquiry to give anything away about what he might know. *"Hi there. This is Greg Denton from the* Washington Review. *I'm trying to find a Brynne Bennett who attended Union Bay High School, San Francisco."*

His message was short and utilitarian, and he left his information for a call back. The history showed he'd only rung her the one time, so there was a very good chance he didn't know much, or if Brynne was even the right person to contact.

I briefed Frances without giving away specific details, told her to look into this Greg Denton at the *Washington Review* and also to see what else she could scrub up in the newspapers I'd bought this morning.

I was just sitting back down, eyeballing my desk drawer where the smokes were stashed, when Neil came in.

"You seem rather . . . human . . . this morning, mate." He sat in the chair and looked me over, a bit of a smirk going on his square jaw.

"Don't say it," I warned.

"A'right." He pulled out his mobile and looked busy with it. "I won't say I know who stayed over last night. And I definitely won't say I saw you two snogging while waiting for the lift this morning on security cam—"

"Piss off!"

Neil laughed at me. "Hell, the office is thrilled, mate. We can all breathe again without fear of disembowelment. The boss got his girl back. Praise the gods!" He looked upward and held his hands up. "It's been a fucked-up couple of weeks—"

"I'd love to see how your miserable arse would do if Elaina suddenly decided she couldn't stand the sight of you." I cut him off, offered up a fake grin and waited for the change in attitude. "Which could always happen, you know, as I know all your shameful secrets."

Worked like a charm. Neil lost the dickhead posturing in about one point five seconds.

"We're really happy for you, E," he said quietly. And I know he meant it.

"How's the military investigation into Lieutenant Oakley going?" I asked, giving in and opening my desk drawer to pull out my lighter and a pack of Djarums.

"He's been doing very bad things to the people of Iraq and getting away with it, but I'm not sure for how long that'll stay buried. I think the senator can only be relieved his son is off getting into trouble in Iraq as opposed to anywhere close to his election campaign."

I grunted in agreement and sucked back my first, sweet inhale. The cloves gave quite a kick, but I was used to it. Now I just let the nicotine do its work and felt guilty for what I was putting into my body. "So he's career military, you think?" I exhaled away from Neil.

Neil shook his head. "I don't think so."

"Why not?"

Neil had the keenest instincts of anyone I knew. He wasn't just an employee, not by a long shot. Neil was much, much more. We'd been boys together, gone off to war, survived that hell to return to England, managing to grow up in the process and start a successful business. I trusted him with my life. Which meant I could trust him with Brynne's as well. I was glad she liked him, because I had the feeling she would have to be guarded eventually whenever she went out. Brynne would so hate that. But even as much as she loathed the security detail, she'd not take it out on Neil. My girl was far too kind for that sort of thing.

I wasn't kidding myself either—friend or no, I was really glad Neil already had a woman, and if he'd been single he wouldn't have been my first choice. He was a good-looking guy.

"Well, this is the interesting part. Lieutenant Lance Oakley was stop-lossed just a few weeks after the plane went down. From what I could find out, the U.S. pretty much ceased with stop-loss over a year ago, and only just a mere handful are served now."

"Are you thinking what I'm thinking, mate?"

Neil nodded again. "As soon as the senator found out he was the next vice presidential hopeful, he got his only son stop-lossed for another tour in Iraq."

I clucked my tongue. "Sounds like the senator knows his son very well and figures the further his boy can keep away from the campaign, the better the senator's chances of being elected." I leaned back in my chair and puffed on my clove. "Who better to get a stop-loss order than somebody who has political connections. I'm starting to think Senator Oakley rather hopes his son never comes back from Iraq. War hero and all that . . . looks smashing for patriotism." I waved my hand for emphasis.

"Precisely where I was going." Neil eyeballed the ciggie in my fingers. "I thought you were cutting back on those."

"I am . . . at home." I stubbed it out into the ashtray. "I won't smoke around her." And I am pretty sure Neil was savvy enough to figure out why I wouldn't. But that was the thing about friends . . . you understood each other, didn't have to explain ad nauseam about painful shit you wished you could forget but pretty much knew was a part of you down to the marrow in your bones.

Brynne's mobile lit up and roused me out of my work. I checked the caller ID. One word—*Mom.*

Well, this ought to be fun, I thought as I pressed send. "Hello."

There was a beat of silence, and then a haughty voice. "I'm trying to reach my daughter, and as I know this is her number, to whom am I speaking?"

"Ethan Blackstone, ma'am."

"Why are you answering my daughter's phone, Mr. Blackstone?"

"I'm surveilling her old number, Mrs.—? I'm sorry, I don't know your name." I wasn't going to give it to her on a silver platter. Brynne's mum would have to ask me. Nicely. So far, I wasn't impressed.

"Exley." She waited for me to say something, but I didn't. I play poker and I know how to wait it out. "Why are you surveilling her phone?"

I couldn't help smiling. We both knew who had won this round. "Yes, well, I deal in security, Mrs. Exley. It's my job. Brynne's dad hired me to see to her safety once Senator Oakley was being vetted. I'm not going to be coy with you either, ma'am. I know why her safety's at risk and so do you. I know everything." Now I paused for effect. "She's told me what happened to her at the hand of Oakley's son."

I heard a sharp inhale and would have paid money to see her face, but alas, I had to use my imagination. "You're the one who bought her portrait, aren't you? She told me about you buying her nude photograph and taking her home after. Something you should know about Brynne, Mr. Blackstone, is that she loves to shock me."

"Is that so? I wouldn't know about that, Mrs. Exley. Brynne's never mentioned you to me before last night. I have nothing to compare you against."

She seemed to ignore my veiled insult and went for the kill. "So you're in a relationship with my daughter, Mr. Blackstone? I can read between the lines and make assumptions as well as the next person. And Brynne is my only child, and contrary to what she's told you, I do love my daughter and only want what's best for her."

"Ethan, please—and yes, I can unequivocally say that I am

in a relationship with Brynne." I reached for a fresh Djarum and flicked my lighter open. Really? This woman didn't know who she was playing with. We could go on like this all day and I would still win. "And I do too."

She was silent a moment and then asked, "You do too what, Mr. Blackstone?"

"Love your daughter and only want what's best for her. I'll keep her safe from any danger. She's my responsibility now."

Again I could only imagine her rolling her eyes at what I'd just said, and I wondered how my girl put up with all the disapproval from this woman. I caught that she didn't take me up on the offer of my first name either. It made me sad for Brynne. Especially since I'd longed for my mum my whole life and here was Brynne with a mum censuring her every decision. I would rather have the loving memory of a mother I'd never had than have to put up with this dragon lady for a lifetime.

"Well then, may I please have her new phone number since she didn't see fit to give it to me herself?" She sounded more like the wounded victim now, and intent upon dismissing me as quickly as possible.

And I was smiling now. I fucking love a winning hand. "Oh please, no, Mrs. Exley, don't take offense. This all happened very suddenly last evening. Brynne told me something yesterday, and I made the decision that she needed a new mobile number. It's that simple. She just hasn't had the time to get in touch with you yet, I am positive that's why." It was easy to be magnanimous when you held the better cards.

"You made the decision, Mr. Blackstone?"

"Yes." Man, my ciggie tasted divine.

"Why are you making those decisions for Brynne?" Mummy had claws, it seemed.

"Because like I said before, Mrs. Exley, I'm going to keep her safe from anyone or anything that tries to hurt her. Anyone . . . or anything." I inhaled a lungful of cloves and savored the taste.

She got quiet then. I waited her out, and eventually she gave in. "Brynne's new number, Mr. Blackstone?"

"Certainly, Mrs. Exley. Tell you what. I'll text her new number to you from my mobile, and that way you can have mine as well. If you have any concerns about this situation with Brynne or any inquiries into her past from media or otherwise, I'd like you to share with me. Please call me any time."

Our conversation wound down very quickly after that and I was more than a tad drained once we hung up. My God, she was difficult. Poor Brynne. Poor Tom Bennett. How in the hell had he ever hooked up with her? Could not see how that relationship ever got off the ground, and I didn't even know what she looked like. I bet she was beautiful, though. Cold, but beautiful.

I texted Brynne's mum with the new number and a short message: **Pleasure chatting with you, Mrs. E. —EB**—and grinned the whole time I was doing it.

Brynne sent me a text about an hour later: **U talked to my mom?! :O**

Oh boy. Mummy had already got to her. I hoped I wasn't in too much trouble. I texted back with: **Sry baby. She rang on ur old mobile and not so happy when I picked up :/**

Brynne hit me right back: **Sorry u had to deal w/ her. I'll make it up to u. ♥♥**

I had to grin at that. I typed: **u gave me 2 ♥'s!! I accept ur offer, baby . . . and she wasn't that bad.** I figured a white lie wasn't going to hurt in regards to my girlfriend's mum. That woman was not nice.

There was a bit of a pause before she responded, but it was worth it when it came through. **U made a big impression on her. I'll tell u later tonight. Have to go to that lunch now. Miss u . . . baby xxx ♥**

I caressed the words on the screen, not wanting to close the message out. She called me baby. She said she missed me. She left me kisses and hearts. I tried not to read too much into it, but still, it was hard not to. I just wanted what I wanted and I didn't want to wait for it a moment longer.

My musings were interrupted when Frances rang in and reminded me I did indeed have a company to run. "I have Ivan Everley on the line for you," she said on speaker.

I told her to put him through and picked up. "You're finding trouble again, aren't you?" I said sarcastically.

"Another death threat came through, E. This time to the World Archery Federation office. I don't give a shit about it, but those fools at the Olympic Commission won't insure a venue for me to announce the competition without some assurance from you. The truly mad are ruling these games, I'm telling you, and I don't have time for this bullshit."

"Don't I know it. I'll speak to them, but I think we should meet to go over the schedule so we can get the security nailed down for you," I told him.

"What are you thinking?"

"I don't know, lunch? I can have Frances set something up for when you're free."

"That should work. I'm really grateful for you, E. Without you, I don't think I'll be announcing at the games at all. Your company pulls some influence with those morons running things."

"Speaking of morons running things . . . Ivan, you've just reminded me of something. Aren't you on the executive board at the National Gallery?"

Ivan snorted. "Yeah, you could say that. Why? And I'll pretend you didn't just insult me because I'm magnanimous like that . . . and family."

"Right, *cousin*." I rolled my eyes. "My girlfriend studies art conservation at University of London. She's American and needs a work visa to stay here indefinitely."

"Wait. Back your arse up. Did you just say your girlfriend? The elusive Blackstone is off the market? How is this possible, mate?"

I should have known I'd get harassed the moment I opened my mouth. I laughed a little awkwardly. "I hardly know, but yeah, she's brilliant at restoring paintings and she really loves what she does. And I *really* don't want her visa expiring . . ."

"I hear you, E. I'll ask. There's this event coming up at the National, actually. The Mallerton Society—"

"Oh yeah, she told me about that. I'm taking her. She been working on one of Mallerton's paintings, actually. I know Brynne can explain it much better than me. I'll introduce her and you'll see what I mean."

"I look forward to meeting the American beauty who snatched your cock off the one-night-stand circuit."

"Please don't tell her that when you meet her or I'll have to look the other way at all those charming death threats you receive so regularly from your loyal fans."

He laughed at me. "You know, if you want her here indefinitely all you have to do is marry her and she won't need a work visa."

My mind went on overcapacity the second he said the words "marry her," and I found myself fumbling for another smoke from the desk drawer.

"You did not just say that to me, even though I shouldn't be surprised, you're such an ignoramus. You of all people endorsing matrimony—that's the most hilarious thing I've heard all year coming from your mouth, or should I say, your idiot arse."

My cousin laughed some more at my expense. "Just because my marriage was an immense cock-up doesn't mean yours will be, E."

"We've definitely reached the end of this conversation, Ivan. I'm hanging up on you now." I could still hear him laughing when I pulled the receiver away from my ear.

Chapter 8

♣ ♠ ♥ ♦

Picking her up from work was something I looked forward to, and today was no exception. Everything was good until that text came through on her mobile. Now I was just plain old desperate to get her in my sights.

I pulled into the Rothvale lot, parked and watched the doors where she would exit the building; my conversation with my cousin still niggled at me since we'd spoken and honestly had infected my imagination with all kinds of madness. *Marriage . . . seriously?!* How about an exclusive, committed relationship for starters?

The idea of marrying anyone had never been on my life list. I just didn't see such a future in my cards and never had. The institution itself held my utmost respect, but in all likelihood a person with my lifestyle and baggage would be most certainly an epic fail as a husband. There was so much shit in my closet, going so far back, that I could hardly think back to a time when I might have turned out normal.

My sister was married, and very happily too, with three beautiful children. Hannah and Freddy were a standard to aspire to, I suppose—I'd just never thought to. My sister had done the domestic route and blessed our dad with grandchildren, and basically gotten me off the hook from having to compete. I mean, Hannah did it so well there was no need for me to feel the pressure.

I decided to call her while I waited for Brynne to come out. I grinned when she picked up on the second ring.

"How's my little brother?"

"Losing his mind with work," I told her.

"That's not the only thing you're losing your mind over, or so I've heard." Hannah could be very smug and annoyingly so when she felt like it.

"So Dad got to you and blabbed already, did he?"

"He's really worried about you. He told me he'd never seen you looking like that, not even when you came home from the war."

"Hmmm. I shouldn't have gone over there and said all that stuff to him. I am such a wanker for doing it. I'll make it up to him somehow. So how are things with my big sis?"

"Good try, E, but I'm not going for it. My brother finally falls in love with someone and you think I am just going to let that juicy tidbit fall away? What do you take me for? We both know who the smartest sibling is here."

I sighed at my sister. "Not arguing with you on that point, Han."

"Wow. You really have changed, haven't you?"

"Yeah, I guess I have. I hope it's for the good. And Dad can stop worrying about me, we're back together now so I'm no longer the wretched, broken creature he last saw."

"Have you been reading poetry, Ethan? You sound different."

"No comment," I said through her sarcasm. "Listen, I wondered if I could bring her up to your place for a weekend. I think Brynne would love Hallborough, and I'd rather like to get her out of the city for a few days. Can you and Freddy squeeze us in?"

"For you? For the chance to meet this American who has transformed my aloof, unattached little brother into a sappy, lovesick drinker of Mexican beers? No problem."

I laughed. "Good. Let me know the dates, Han. I want all of you to meet her, and your lovely home would be the perfect place to do that. And I miss the kids."

"They miss their uncle Ethan. Okay . . . I'll check the books and let you know when. It's starting to get busier with the Games coming."

"You don't have to tell me that. The whole city's gone mad and we're just in June!"

We hung up and I looked out the window, waiting for Brynne. I pulled out her mobile from my pocket and brought up the text that had ruined my otherwise peaceful day. Some bloke named Alex Craven from the Victoria and Albert Museum that I would just love to turn into a eunuch: **Brynne, Lovely seeing you again today. Brill on the Mallerton too. I'd very much love to take you to dinner and discuss further how**

we can get you on staff. Didn't know you modeled but now I've seen your pictures I must know more! –Alex

I am sure I cut the side of my tongue from gritting my teeth together. The urge to reply back was something I wanted to do so badly I could taste it next to the tang of blood in my mouth—along the lines of: **Sod off, you idiot tosser. She's taken and her man will cut off your balls if you so much as think about her naked. –Ethan w/ the big knife.**

Of course I didn't, but just barely.

God, how to handle myself? I was no bloody good at this sort of thing. Jealousy sucked, and I would be in for a shitload with Brynne—part of the package with her, when she was so beautiful and on display so prominently. I needed more reassurance from her, and I was pretty sure she wasn't ready for giving me any more just yet.

The passenger door opened and in she came, plopping onto the seat, flushed from a dash through the light drizzle that'd started in the time since I had parked. She grinned and leaned toward me for a kiss.

"Well, there you are," I said and pulled her against me. Her skin was a little cold, but her lips were warm and soft for me.

Fuck yes, for me!

I plundered that mouth of hers and held her face to mine, claiming her with my tongue deeply so she could feel how much I wanted her. She allowed the invasion at first and I didn't let up until she squeaked, telling me I needed to back off. I released her and leaned to the side in my seat to look at her.

"Sorry, that was a little beastly of me." I gave her my best chastised look.

Her face changed and her eyes got that searching look

in them. Christ, she was beautiful. No wonder cocksuckers named Alex wanted her naked. *I* wanted her naked. Like right fucking now! Her hair was down today and she had on a dark green jacket and a scarf. The color was lovely on her, picking up the green and hazel in her eyes, and she had a few drops of rain sprinkled in her hair.

"What's wrong, Ethan?"

"Why do you think something's wrong?"

"Just a really good hunch," she smirked, "and the tongue lashing confirmed it."

I shook my head. "I just missed you is all. How was your luncheon with those colleagues you wanted to impress?"

"It was awesome. I got to share about Lady Percival's restoration, and it really gave them a hook to remember me by. I hope something comes of it. Maybe it will." She smiled. "And I owe it all to you." She kissed me once on the lips and took my chin in her hand.

I tried to smile back. I thought I did, but apparently I suck at faking my feelings just as much as I suck at dealing with my jealousy. *Oh, something will come of it, baby. Alex Craven will get a hard-on and the hook will be remembering your naked pictures, not the soulful Lady Percival holding her rare and precious book! Mallerton's paintings can go to rot, it's Brynne Bennett on his cock that he wants!*

She sighed at me. "Are you going to tell me what's wrong? You just growled, and I'm pretty sure growling is not a universal signal for happiness and harmony." She looked very annoyed with me.

"This came through a bit ago." I set her mobile on her lap with the text on screen.

She picked it up and read it, swallowed once and then looked sideways at me. "You got jealous when you saw this." Not a question.

I nodded at her. Might as well let it all hang out while we were at it. "He wants to fuck you."

All men do when they see your nude photographs. I wasn't moronic enough to say that to her, but man I could sure think it if I wanted. It was the bare-naked truth!

"I highly doubt that, Ethan."

"Is he gay, then?"

She shrugged. "I don't think Alex is gay, but I don't really know."

"Then he definitely wants to fuck you," I said grimly out the window now coated with drizzle and setting a mood in perfect harmony with how I felt.

"Ethan, look at me."

The tone of her command shocked the hell out of me. And got me hard.

I looked over at my girl, who had come to mean so much to me in such a short time, and wondered what she wanted to say. I didn't know how to share her, or how to not be jealous, or how to be the graceful partner of a nude art model that other men only wanted to drool over or fantasize about fucking. I just didn't know how to be that man.

"Alex Craven is not a *he*."

Brynne rolled her lips together to keep from laughing outright. It didn't matter. I was relieved enough to take her teasing and then some.

"Oh," I managed, feeling very, very foolish, "well then, you *should* go to dinner with Alex Craven and I'll wish you a ton of luck, baby. She sounds like she really wants to hire you." I nodded.

She laughed at me and said, "You worry far too much, baby."

I leaned toward her lips but didn't touch them. "I can't help worrying, and I love it when you call me baby." I kissed her again, this time not like a Neanderthal, but how I should have kissed her in the first place. I threaded my fingers around her head and tried to show her what she meant to me. I pulled back slowly with a few nibbles to her bottom lip, bringing my hand down the side of her face and down her neck. "I want to take you home now. My place. I need that . . . badly."

I hope she knew this was my version of a request. I'd asked her to bring enough clothes for a few days but couldn't be sure she'd actually done it. I just wanted her with me all the time. I couldn't explain it any differently than a very deep wanting . . . a requirement of having her right there for me to talk to and touch. And fuck. It made me such a needy bastard, but I just didn't care anymore, and holding back from pushing her was annoyingly difficult.

"All right, your place tonight." She brought her hand up to my hair and fingered it, searching me again with her intelligent eyes. I swear she could read me like an open book, and I wondered why she even put up with me. I hoped it was because she was beginning to love me back, but I hated to ponder much because I always returned to . . . *what if she doesn't?*

"Thank you." I took her hand from where she held it and brought it to my lips to kiss. I lifted my eyes to see her reaction and was pretty damn happy to see that smile of hers. I smiled back and put the car in drive. Time to get my girl home alone, where I could act on all those things I really wanted to do with her.

The chicken parmigiana in my mouth was perfectly prepared with succulent meat, savory sauce and spices, but the company sitting across from me at my table was even better.

I'd watched her make it earlier while I worked from my laptop. Sort of. I'd come out and set up on the kitchen bar and got to look over and smile at her sometimes. I enjoyed the sounds of her working in the kitchen very much. It was a nice feeling, combined with the delicious smells coming from a room I rarely spent much time in. Smells of our dinner that Brynne was making with her lovely hands.

Pretty fucking sexy stuff if you ask me.

It was different than what Annabelle did for me—an employee who cleaned and cooked things and labeled them in the freezer. This was something real. A thing people do because they care, not because they are being paid.

Having a woman in my home cooking for me was not something I had any experience with either. But I was pretty sure I could get used to it. Yup. Brynne had me hooked. Brilliant, sexy, beautiful, accomplished, a damn fine cook—and beyond fine spread out underneath me in my bed. Did I mention sexy and beautiful? I thought about bedtime for us later.

I took another bite and savored the taste. She had her hair up in one of those claw clips and a deep V-necked top in crimson that drew my eyes right down to her mouthwatering nipples, which were budded up nicely and screaming for my mouth. A few long strands of hair had slipped from her hair clip and rested over the swells of her cleavage. *Mmmmm, delicious.*

"I'm glad you think so. This is really simple to make," she said.

I watched her mouth and lips as she took a sip of wine, totally shocked I had spoken aloud and glad she thought I was merely talking about the food. "How did you learn to cock so well?" I sputtered, "I mean cook!"

She rolled her eyes and shook her head.

I gave her a grin and a wink. "You do *both* so well, baby, my cock *and* the cooking part."

"You idiot," she scolded. "I watched cooking shows and learned. My dad let me experiment on him after the divorce. You can ask him about when I first started cooking." She laughed and speared another bite of dinner and popped it into her mouth. "But better not ask him about when I started *cocking* you!"

I laughed at myself and hung my head. "Not as good as this food you've made tonight, then?"

"Not even close. My first attempts were awful, and Daddy paid the price. He never complained, though."

"Your dad is no fool, and he loves you so very much."

"I'm glad you two talked it out. He really does like you, Ethan. He respects you a lot." She smiled at me.

"Ahhh, well, I feel the same about him." I hesitated before bringing up her mum, but figured I should. "I don't think your mum was too impressed with me today, though. Sorry about that. I thought it best to introduce myself and tell her what I was doing in your life—I probably could have said it more tactfully, though."

She shook her head. "It's okay. She actually said she's glad you're watching out for me, and that you sounded determined to make sure nothing happens . . ."

I caught the falter in her voice and wanted nothing more than to reassure her, but I waited for her to finish.

"She thinks you're obsessed with me, though." Brynne toyed with her chicken.

I shrugged. "I didn't hold back with her, it's true. I told your mum how I feel about you."

She smiled at me. "She told me that too. Pretty brave of you, Ethan."

"Telling the truth is not brave, it's expected." I shook my head. "It's important to me that your parents know I'm not just providing security for their daughter." I reached a hand toward her. "It's important that you know that too, Brynne, because you're so much more to me."

She put her hand into mine and I gripped it, closing my eyes, and closing my fingers around the delicate bones of her hand. The same lovely hand that had made my dinner tonight, and tied my tie this morning. The same hand that would be touching my body when I took her to bed and laid her out a very short while from now.

"You are too, Ethan."

I felt that possessiveness come over me again. I swear it worked like a switch. One minute I was tolerating our situation well, or thought I was, and then something was spoken, or alluded to, and bam, I went into I-need-to-fuck-you-now land.

Her words were all I needed to hear. I rose up from my chair and took her with me, picking her up with my arms and feeling those long legs of hers wrap around my waist so I could carry her out of the dining room and into the bedroom.

She held the sides of my face and kissed me madly the whole way I carried her. I wasn't complaining. I loved it when she was all sexed up. And Brynne could be like that.

Thank. Fuck.

I peeled her top and bottoms off her, not waiting for the foreplay of stripping, needing to see her body before I totally lost it. She had on a violet bra and a black thong. I groaned down at her from above. "What are you trying to do, woman, kill me?"

She smiled and slowly shook her head back and forth. "Never," she whispered.

I leaned down and kissed her slow and sweet for that answer, but my heart was beating hard and fast. God, I loved how she was with me, so soft and alluring—accepting of me.

I loved many things about her.

I flipped her over onto her stomach and unhooked that pretty bra and ditched the thong. I just took in the sight and breathed out, dragging my hands down her back, her hips, the cheeks of her lovely bum and then back up again.

Once she was naked, I calmed some and slowed it down. I left my clothes on and stretched out beside her. She turned her face to mine and we just stared at each other.

I reached for the hair clip and took it away, spreading her hair out on her back and shoulders. Brynne had long, silky hair. I loved to touch it and drag my fingers through pieces of it. I loved when it whipped my chest when she was on top of me working out my cock. I loved to grab a huge handful and hold her with it while I fucked her to a shattering orgasm and she cried out my name.

But I didn't do any of that tonight. Instead I worked her over slowly and carefully, getting into all the places I have to be with my tongue and my fingers, making her come and come again before I got undressed and got my cock into her.

We fit beautifully together like this. Sex with her shattered me down to my deepest levels of complexity; even if Brynne wasn't aware, I was. I don't even know what I said to her during the heat of it. I say all kinds of things to her because she likes my filthy mouth. She told me so. It's a damn good thing too because I cannot help it. The filter between my brain and my mouth is pretty much nonexistent.

I still didn't know what I said to her after the explosive orgasm that had me so drained I began drifting off to sleep still buried inside her and hoping she let me stay there for a while.

But I knew it when she said, "I love you too."

My eyes flew open and I stared into the dark and held on to her. I replayed the sound of those words over and over and over again.

Fuck. They're going to do it. My heart started to pump as fear like I'd never known raced on adrenaline-charged veins throughout my body. I'd been waiting for this to come. Deep down I knew it would, but to save my sanity I'd pushed it away. Denial worked for a while but the time for that had expired.

"Are you ready?" he asked me. The creature who asked the question was the one I wanted to gut and leave to leak out slowly. The one who talked about HER. The one who taunted all the time about hurting her.

Fuck, NOOOOO!

I shook my head as he advanced on me, his face very close, the smoke from his clove handrolled swirling and tantalizing, making my mouth water. Funny how I could crave a cigarette in a moment like this, but I did. I would've pulled the fuckin' thing out of his mouth and shoved it in mine if I could've.

My arms were pinned from behind by another and my nose plugged. I tried to hold my breath and go out that way but my body betrayed me. The second I gasped in a breath he poured something vile down my throat. I tried to keep the elixir from going down, but again my body took over in a basic function to keep me breathing. How ironic. They were drugging me in order to execute me . . . so I wouldn't fight the process . . . so they could videotape my death and show it around the world.

No. No! NO!

I fought it with everything I possessed but he just laughed at my efforts. I felt tears squeeze out of my eyes but I was sure I wasn't crying. I never cried.

He barked out the order and then I saw it. The camera. A subordinate set it up on a tripod while I stared and let the tears roll out as the opium started its hold upon me.

I was indeed crying, I realized.

But not for the reasons they thought. I cried for my dad and for my sister. For my girl. They would have to see this . . . thing . . . be done to me. The whole world would watch. She would see.

"Introduce yourself!" *he ordered.*

I shook my head and gestured to the camera. "No video! No VIDEO, you cocksucker! NO FUCKING VIDEO—"

The backhand across my mouth was so brutal it shut me up by force of the blow. He barked another order at the one with the video camera, who aimed the lens at my tags and read in halting English: "Blackstone, E. SAS. Captain. Two nine one five zero one."

He started toward me again, and this time he pulled a kukri out of its sheath. The blade was curved and finely honed. Even in my drug-weakened ability to react to what was coming, I could see the tool was well prepared for the job it was about to do.

I thought of my mum. I'd wanted her all my life and now more than ever. I wasn't brave. I was afraid to die. What would happen to Brynne? Who would protect her from them once I was gone?

Oh, God . . .

"No video. No video. No video. No video," was all I could utter. And if the sound was no longer an utterance capable via my mouth, then it would be the last thing in my mind along with "I'm so sorry, Dad. Hannah. Brynne . . . I'm so fucking sorry!"

"Ethan! Baby, wake up. You're having a dream." The sweetest voice met my ears and the softest hands touched me.

I bolted up gasping, consciousness cranking me into a state of hyper-alertness. Her hands fell away as I slammed into the headboard and sucked in oxygen. Poor Brynne, eyes wide, looked horrified as she sat up with me in bed.

"Oh, fuck!" I panted, accepting the reality of where I was.

Breathe, motherfucker!

I'd done this many times. It was only in my head. Not real. But here I sat, losing my shit royally in front of my girl. It had to be scary for her and I regretted that deeply. I felt like I might be sick.

She reached out again, the cool touch of her hand on my chest grounding me, bringing me back to the here and now. Brynne was right here next to me in the bed, not in that fucked-up dream again. I kept bringing her into my nightmares. Why in the hell was I doing that?

She scooted closer and I clutched at her hand on my chest, needing her touch like a lifeline.

"What was that about, Ethan? You were shouting stuff and thrashing all over the place in the bed. I couldn't wake you—"

"What did I say?" I cut her off.

"Ethan," she said soothingly, reaching for my face, her fingers grazing my jaw.

"What did I say?" I yelled, grabbing her hand and holding it out from my body, feeling the urge to retch at the thought of what might have come out of my mouth. She flinched back and my heart broke for frightening her, but I had to know. I stared at her in the dark and tried to take in enough oxygen to fill my lungs. A nearly pointless exercise, though. There wasn't enough air in all of London to satisfy me right now.

"You were saying 'No video' over and over. What does *that* mean, Ethan?"

The sheet had fallen down to her waist, baring her lovely naked breasts in the glow of the moon peeking through the skylights. I saw a wariness in her eyes as she tugged her hand out of my grip, and I hated it. I let her go.

"I'm sorry. I—I have dreams sometimes. Sorry for shouting at you." I lurched out of bed and into the bathroom. I hung over the sink and let the water flow over my head, rinsed my mouth and drank from the faucet. Fuck, I needed to get my shit together—this was so not right. I had to be strong for her. All that stuff was ancient history and buried in the hell of my past. It was not welcome in my present and sure as hell not in my future with Brynne.

Her arms wrapped around me from behind. I could feel her naked against my back, and it woke my cock up. She pressed her lips to my scars and kissed. "Talk to me. Tell me what that was back there." Her soft voice carried the strength of steely determination, but there was no way I could bring her into that tortured mess.

No fucking way she's going there with me. Not her innocent self.

"No. I don't want to." I looked into the mirror over the sink and saw myself, water dripping off my hair, Brynne's arms still around me, her hands resting on my chest where my heart was pounding mercilessly from an immense nightmare of all kinds of fucked up. Yet she was holding me, holding my heart in her beautiful hands. She'd followed me in here to comfort me.

"What video, Ethan? You kept screaming about a video."

"I'm not talking about it!" I closed my eyes at the sound of my voice against hers, hating the anger in it, hating she had to see me like this.

"Was it because of me? The video of me?" She took her hands away and backed off me. "You said you never saw it." I could hear the hurt in her voice and imagined where her mind was going with this scenario. She couldn't be more off the mark.

I lost it then, totally and completely, fearful she might not trust me, terrified she would leave again. I spun around and pulled her against me hard. "No, baby. Not that. Please. It's not that. It's me—from the past—a bad time for me in the war."

"You won't tell, though. Why can't you say what happened to you—your scars. Ethan?"

She tried to pull away, to make distance between us, but hell if I would allow it. "No, Brynne, I need you. Don't pull away from me."

"I'm not—"

I cut her words off with my mouth crushed against hers, owning her with my tongue so deep all she could do was take it. I picked her up and stumbled to the bed with her. I had to be inside her, in every way. I needed the validation that she was here, that I was alive, that she was safe in my care, that I was alive . . . that she was safe . . . that I was alive . . .

"Baby, you're so beautiful and good for me. You're fucking everything to me, okay? Tell me that you want me." I was babbling as I pushed her legs apart with my knees and got two fingers inside her wet heat. I started stroking, working all that spunk from before all around and over her clit the way she liked.

"I want you, Ethan," she answered breathily, her sex heating up for me, ready to take me in. God, I battled the razor's edge of control when she got all submissive with me—the ultimate turn-on even though she was really the first woman where it worked like that.

"Tell me you'll let me have all of you. Every part. I want it all, Brynne!"

"I'll let you!" she cried out. "I'm right here."

I speared into her mouth again, deep and thorough with my tongue, my fingers moving inside her pussy, getting her wetter still. "Your mouth is mine when you wrap those raspberry lips around my cock and suck me off."

She moved underneath me. I dragged away from her lips to latch onto a nipple. I bit down enough to get the moan out of her then sucked deep to plump it back up before doing the same to the other breast. "Your beautiful tits belong to me too. When I bite on them and suck and drive you mad."

"Oh, God."

I moved down her body, my fingers still up in her, sliding along her nub, getting her closer to climax. "This sweet honey cunt is always mine when I cram it full of my cock and blow a load of cum up into it." I whispered more filthy talk and felt sure it got her hotter.

She writhed and rolled her head around and I loved that I was making her wild.

I flicked my tongue over her clit and even put my teeth on it, nipping her flesh until I heard her cry and switched to soothing, ever so gently with a soft touch, stringing her out further and further.

"I need more! Fuck me, Ethan!"

Oh yeah, she was hotter.

Holy hell, I finally had my girl right where I wanted her. I went mad with the taste of her all over my tongue, my taste, her scent, her warmth, the soaking wet, octane-fueled sex!

"I can give you more, baby. I want to give you more." I pulled my fingers out of her quim, sliding them back to her other hole, and rimmed the opening with my drenched index finger. She gasped in a breath and stilled. I lifted my head and moved up her body, one arm propping me, the other hand free to explore. I slipped just my fingertip inside and met her gaze. She looked wild, her eyes flaring. "I want in here, Brynne. Will you let me fuck your beautiful arse?" I spoke up against her quivering lips and bit on the bottom one, my fingertip still teasing her entrance, waiting for her answer.

"Yes!" It came out a harsh whisper but definitely agreement.

I pulled away and flipped her onto her stomach. I gripped her hips up in the air and split her legs wide so I could get to her from on my knees. She was stunning. Totally spread for me, anticipating and accepting and off-the-charts perfect.

My hand on my shaft, I slid the head around her drenched sex, working it over her clit again and again, getting her closer to coming and my cock well lubed.

"Mmm-hmm," I groaned, centering the bell end against her tight hole. "You are something so fucking perfect . . ." I pushed and penetrated just the tip of my cock, trying to open her up a bit, and thought I could easily lose it. As in ejaculating before I ever got inside her.

She tensed and arched from my invasion, so I eased up immediately, putting my palm on her lower back to steady her. "Easy, relax for me, baby." She stilled and breathed heavily, waiting on me, submitting to my desires; so perfectly takeable and gloriously tight with her muscle gripping around the head of my ready-to-blow cock. I didn't want to hurt her, but my God, what a spectacular turn-on to be poised like I was, about to claim that final place where I could meld into her.

She quivered beneath me. "You're about to make me come, baby. I want to so badly, but you first. I'm gonna make you feel so good!"

"Ethan, please make me come!" She squirmed against my just-tipped cock ready to take me all the way. I realized she would allow me in even if it was painful because she was such a generous lover.

Saints help me!

It took everything I had not to sink into that stretched, mysterious part of her I had yet to claim. I wanted to. I needed to. But I wanted and needed to cherish her more. I knew I would hurt her and she was nowhere near ready. We'd have to work up to it—something to look forward to. Like any new thing we did together. I was out of my fucking mind right now and this was not the moment to push her into anal for the first time with me.

"Brynne, I love you so much," I whispered against her back, notching my cock down to find her pussy. The flesh was so hot it burned when we touched. I heard my own shout when I slammed deep inside her and started to fuck. My hands on her hips gripped tight, knocking her back hard onto my shaft, again and again and again, the sounds of our bodies slapping amid grunts as pure pleasure took over from there.

We were at it for a long time. I needed that terrorized dream out of my system and fucking was a way for me to make that happen. If you can fuck, then you are alive—the brutal logic was fairly hard to dispute there.

It was pretty rough shagging too, even for us. And Brynne could take it rough from me. She had before and she would again because I'd never let her go. Never. I couldn't imagine doing the things I'd just done to her with anyone else. I knew I wouldn't be able to.

I understood later in the dark, after the crazed sex trip I'd dragged her on, and after she fell into a deep sleep beside me. She'd come so many times she just passed out from exhaustion once I could finally bring myself to stop. She never asked me to stop, though. My girl gave herself to me and didn't press for answers. And I was glad because I didn't want to talk about any of it yet. My insides were far too raw after my nightmare.

I wanted to light up but denied myself. It felt wrong in regards to her. It was wrong to subject her to my unhealthful smoking and I wouldn't do it around her anymore.

Watching her sleeping after that session, her methodical breathing, her long lashes resting above her cheekbones, her hair swirling wildly over the pillow, completely took my breath away. I knew I had found my angel at last and I would hold on to her with everything I had.

No more yielding but a dream . . .

She saved me from the utter madness of my torment. She made me want things I'd never wanted before. I would kill if I had to in order to keep her safe. It would kill me if anything ever happened to her.

Eventually I was able to fall asleep again, and it was only because she was right there with me.

Chapter 9

I woke up to an empty bed and an empty flat, and an authentic nightmare. After what happened in the night, the last thing I expected was for Brynne to go AWOL on me.

My first clue that something wasn't right came when I rolled over in the bed and kept going. No soft, warm body smelling of flowers and the decadent shagging from last night to press against and wrap myself around. Just sheets and pillows. She wasn't in my bed. I called out her name and got only ominous silence back. I began to feel sickening dread.

Last night too much for her?

I checked the bathroom first. I could see she'd used the shower. Her cosmetics and brush were out on the vanity, but she was definitely absent. Not in the kitchen making coffee, not in my office checking her emails, not working out in the gym, not *anywhere* inside the flat.

I pulled up the security camera video on a monitor that recorded the front door and hallway. Anyone coming or going would be on it. My heart pounded so hard my chest had to be visibly moving. I rewound the last hour and there she was, dressed in joggers and trainers heading for the lifts, headphones stuck in her ears.

"Fuck!" I screamed, slamming my hand down on my desktop. Out for a morning run? Un-fucking-believable. I blinked at what I was seeing and scrubbed a hand over my beard.

"Tell me you're on her right now!" I shouted into the direct line to Neil.

"What?" He sounded like he was still laid up in bed, and I felt more ill than before.

"Wrong answer, mate. Brynne's left the flat. On a run!"

"I was sleeping, E," he said. "Why would I be tagging her if she's in the flat with you—"

I hung up on Neil and rang Brynne on her mobile. It went to voice mail, of course. I almost threw my phone at the wall but I managed to text her with: **WTF RU?**

I ran to my closet, threw on some clothes and shoes, grabbed car keys, wallet, mobile, and bailed down to the garage. I tore out onto the street, tires squealing, and started calculating how far she could have gone in the time since she'd been tracked on security cam, my mind running wild with scenarios of how easy it would be for a professional hit to take her out at this hour and make it look like an accident.

It was early, just past seven, a typical overcast London morning coming alive for the day. The usual delivery vans and street vendors moving about, the neighborhood coffee-house doing a brisk business, a few early-morning runners getting their workouts in, but not the one I was looking for. She could be anywhere.

I kept coming back to why she would take off without telling me. I was scared shitless it was because of me. What she'd seen of me last night. What had happened after . . . I was in so far over my head with Brynne it was laughable. God knows we both have our issues, but maybe that clusterfuck of emotions last night was more than she wanted to put up with. I rubbed my chest and kept driving.

My mobile rang. Neil. I put him through the in-car speakers.

"I've not spotted her yet. I'm on Cromwell now, heading south, but I think I've traveled further than she could've since the time stamp on the security cam."

"Look, E, I'm sorry."

"You can tell me that after I find her." I was angry, but it wasn't his fault. Brynne had been with me and Neil was technically off duty. My fault. What a fucking mess.

"I'll head east, then. Lots of joggers follow Heath Downs by the park."

"Do that, mate."

I kept scanning, praying for the sight of her, when a text came through: **Ur up. Gettin coffee. What u want me 2 bring u?**

How about your sweet arse at home, woman!

The relief absolutely brought me to my knees in gratitude, but I was so very angry at her for this stunt. Out getting bloody coffee! Sweet Christ! I pulled over immediately and just rested my head on the steering wheel for a moment. I so needed to sit her down and explain a few things about how her life would have to change over the next few months. And that solo morning runs were definitely off the menu.

Bugger me!

My fingers shook as I texted: **Which coffee shop?**

A short pause and then: **Hot Java. R U mad???**

Ignorant question.

The coffee shop she named was the one not more than a block from my flat. We'd even gone there together a few mornings when she'd stayed the night with me. Brynne had been right close to home the whole time! I texted back: **Don't leave!! Comin 2 get u!**

It took at least ten minutes to navigate the roads back to my neighborhood. I was angry at myself—for several reasons, but mostly for sleeping through her waking up and leaving without my knowledge. I'd been in such a rush going after her that I'd passed right by her in the coffee shop, and that was just unacceptable. I was slipping.

I decided to put the reasons for my deep sleeping aside for the time being.

Nightmare from hell and resulting shag-a-thon, maybe?

Oh, I knew it'd be dredged up again in conversation at some point, probably soon, because Brynne would ask me, but right now I was just too raw to face what was bubbling up from my subconscious. Denial looked so much more attractive.

Fuck me running! Pun intended.

Fucking hell, if she wasn't in the shop like I'd told her to be but out on the sidewalk holding two coffees! And she wasn't alone either. Some bloke was all over her, chatting her up, who knows who the fuck he was to her. Somebody she knew? Or someone feeling her out for God only knows what purpose! She was so getting spanked for this stunt when I got her alone.

I had to park on the opposite side of the road and then cross. She spotted me approaching and said something to her companion, who looked over at me. His eyes flared a bit and he sidled up closer to her.

Wrong fucking move, arsehole.

"Ethan," she said, smiling as if this was a perfectly acceptable way to start the day.

Oh, my darling, we very much need to have a talk about things.

"Brynne," I said tightly, pulling her into me at the waist and getting a good, long look at her *friend,* who needed to be on his merry way like ten minutes ago. The guy was a little too bold for my tastes, standing there like he was entitled to be talking to her, like he'd done it before and had history with her. Shit! He knew her. This man knew Brynne.

"Ethan, this is Paul Langley, umm, a friend from the art department. He teaches . . . I was just leaving and there was Paul coming in."

She was nervous. Brynne looked uncomfortable, and if I was good at anything, it was reading people. I could smell the unease coming off her. Now, the bloke was a different story. He looked far too smug and a bit too entitled, which was how I figured it out.

Brynne seemed to catch herself and said, "Paul, this is Ethan . . . Blackstone, my boyfriend." She handed me one of the coffees. "I got you a misto." She looked at me and took a sip from her cup. Yep. She was uncomfortable.

The plonker stuck his hand out and offered first.

I hate you.

I had one arm around Brynne and the other hand occupied with the coffee she'd just palmed off on me. I would need to let her go in order to shake. I despised him in his slick suit, professional, clean cut and, from all appearances, plenty of brass. I unwound my hand from around Brynne's waist and accepted his grip. I squeezed firm and tried not to think about how bloody awful I looked, which was exactly like I'd just fallen out of bed.

"A pleasure," Langley said, not meaning it.

I returned the briefest nod. It was the best I could do and I didn't really give a shit whether I was being rude or not. He was a bloke in the wrong place at the wrong time to ever be a friend of mine. I loathed him on sight.

His eyes flicked over me. I decided I would be the one to end this handshake first. Or pissing contest, as it were.

I withdrew my hand and pressed my lips to Brynne's hair, but I kept my eyes on him as I spoke. "I woke up and you were gone." I drew my arm back around her.

She laughed nervously. "I just felt like a white chocolate mocha this morning."

"You still need your morning coffee, I see. Some things never change, eh, Brynne darling?" Langley grinned conspiratorially at Brynne, and in that instant I knew. He'd fucked her. Or tried his best to. They had some sort of history, and I could only see the red rag of jealousy being dangled in front of my eyes. Holy fucking hell, the violent emotions that washed through me in those seconds. I wanted to show Langley the way down to the sidewalk face-first with my fist, but I needed to get her away from him even more.

"Time to go, baby," I announced, pressing my hand at her back.

Brynne stiffened for an instant but then gave in. "It was so nice to see you again, Paul. You take care."

"Same to you, darling. I've got your new number and you have mine, so you know where to find me, all right?" The bastard looked at me and there was no mistaking the challenge in his gaze. He thought I was some sort of meathead and was throwing out a dare to me that if Brynne needed rescuing she had only to call and Prince Charming would come for her.

Sod. Off. You. Pathetic. Prick.

Brynne nodded and smiled at him. "Good-bye, Paul."

Yeah, bugger off . . . Paul.

It was so apparent that Lover Paul did not want to leave her. He wanted to kiss her or hug her in some show of an affectionate farewell but had brains enough not to try it. I didn't say he was stupid, just my enemy.

"I'll call you. I want to hear all about the Mallerton." He did a hand to the ear gesture. "Bye, darling." He gave me a look and I gave him one right back. I truly hoped he could read minds, because I had so much worth saying that he really needed to hear.

You cock-swinging, worthless shit bag! You will absolutely NOT call her to talk about the Mallerton. You won't look at her and you won't think about her either! Got it?! My girl is NOT your darling now, nor will she ever be in the future. Get out of my sight before I'm forced to do something that will land me into a fuckload of trouble with MY girl.

We started across the street, my heart pounding, the anger just pouring out of me, when she opened her mouth.

"What in the hell was all that back there, Ethan? You were incredibly rude."

"Keep walking. We'll discuss this at home," I managed to grit out as we crossed.

She glared at me like I'd grown a second head and stopped on the sidewalk. "I asked you a question. Don't talk to me like I'm a child who's in trouble!"

"Get in the car," I snapped, trying to keep from picking her up and setting her in the seat, which was dangerously close to happening even if she didn't know it yet.

"Excuse me, but this is bullshit. I'm walking back!" She flounced away from me.

I wanted to explode, I was so pissed. I grabbed her hand to keep her from leaving. "No, you are not walking back, Brynne. Get in the car now. I'm taking you home." I spoke low and right into her face, where I could see her angry eyes flashing up at me. She was so stunning when she was riled. She made me want to drag her into my bed and do very naughty things to her body for about a day and a half.

"I'm not being ordered by you. Why are you acting like this?"

I closed my eyes and called for patience. "I'm not acting at all." People were looking at us. Could probably hear our conversation too. Bloody hell! "Would you *please* get yourself in the car, Brynne?" I forced a fake smile.

"You are being such a prick, Ethan. I still have a life. I am going running in the mornings and can stop at the coffee shop if I want to."

"Not without me or Neil, you aren't. Now, get your sweet Yank arse in the motherfucking car!"

She stared at me for a moment and shook her head, eyes blazing daggers at me. Her chin lifted imperiously before she stomped over to the Rover and got in. I ignored her behavior, thinking I was being pretty damn magnanimous in the circumstances. I texted Neil to let him know I had her and made her wait on me while I did it. She was locked inside the car and couldn't go anywhere—for the moment, at least.

I looked at her. She looked at me. She was angry with me. I was beyond enraged with her.

"Don't you *ever* do that again," I told her in no uncertain terms.

"What, walk? Buy a coffee?" She pouted and looked out the window. Her mobile lit up and buzzed. She looked over at me as she accepted the call. "Yes, I'm fine, Paul. I apologize for whatever that was, but no worries. Just a little lovers' spat." She actually smirked at me as she told that puffed-up cocksucker I was having a bad day.

I wanted to rip the mobile out of her hands and throw it out the window, and I probably would have if she had not turned it off and put it away in a pocket. "You know what I mean, Brynne, and don't fucking mock me to him!"

"You embarrassed me back there, Ethan! Paul thinks you are—"

"I don't give a maiden queen's first fuck what that cocksucker thinks! What is he to you, anyway?"

"He's a nice guy and a friend." She wouldn't look me in the eye when she said it, and I knew. Oh fuck, did I know!

"Did you let him fuck you, Brynne? Has he knowledge of that fanny of yours that was just made for shagging? Has he had his hands all over you, his cock inside you? Hmmmm? I really want to know. Tell me about you and nice guy Paul."

"You are such an asshole right now." She folded her arms beneath her breasts and looked forward out the windscreen. "I'm not telling you anything."

"Did you fuck him!?"

She shifted in the seat and gave me a look that made pain shoot up my cock. "Who did you nail last before you turned your sights on me, Ethan? Who was that lucky girl? I know it couldn't have been more than a week past when we got it on for the first time!" She started waving her hands in gestures. "Said the guy who thinks a week is a long time to go without some sex!"

Well, shit!

That wasn't a nice thought, because she was right. I hated to admit it, but I couldn't tell her the name of the last one who'd been able to get me up for it. Pamela? Penelope? Something with a *P*. Ivan would know, he had a long list of female *friends* and he'd introduced us. I scowled at the realization that I couldn't really remember and the fact that whoever she'd been hadn't made her or the shagging any more memorable than the letter of her name.

Paul started with a *P* as well, I thought. I was quite certain I'd never forget his name, though.

"Having trouble remembering her name?" Brynne asked.

Yes.

"What color was her hair, hmmm?"

Strawberry blonde, au naturale. I do remember that much.

"Were you going to fuck her again, Ethan, if you hadn't met me?" she kept taunting.

I didn't answer. I started the car and pulled out into traffic, just wanting to get home and maybe back to where we'd been only a few hours ago. I hated arguing with her.

"Why did you slip out?" I managed finally. "After last night, you just ditched me this morning?"

"I did not ditch you, Ethan. I got up, used your treadmill, took a shower and wanted a mocha coffee. We go to that shop all the time and I knew you were tired from . . . um . . . last night."

So she was thinking about last night too. I didn't yet know if this was to my advantage or not, but I hoped so. I pulled into the garage of my building and parked the Rover. I looked over at her hissing mad in the seat.

Brynne wasn't finished chewing me out, apparently. "It's something I do most every morning. It wasn't raining and the day was perfect for a short walk down to the corner." She threw up her hands again. "I had my run on the treadmill and wanted to get a white chocolate mocha. Is that such a crime? It's not like I busted into the Tower and nabbed the crown jewels or something."

I rolled my eyes. "Baby, do you have any idea what it was like for me this morning to find you gone? No message, no note, no nothing!"

She threw her head back onto the seat and looked up. "God help me! I left you a note! I did. I set it on my pillow so you'd see. It said: *Went to get coffee at Java. Be back soon.* I used *your* gym and took a shower before I left. Doesn't that speak to what I was doing? Nothing covert going on, just having a normal morning, Ethan!"

Not the kind of normal I want to wake up to ever again, thank you very much!

"I didn't get your blasted note! I rang you and got voice mail! Why didn't you pick up if you were just in line for coffees?" I got out and wrenched open her door. I wanted her back in the flat in private. This public brawling sucked.

She shook her head at me and got out of the car. "I was talking to my aunt Marie."

I stabbed at the lift call button. "At that hour of the morning?" I ushered her into the lift and backed her into a corner, my arms caging her in where I could get a little more influence over her. She was a loose cannon at the moment. The sound of the doors closing us into privacy was the most welcome sound I'd heard in the last minutes.

"Aunt Marie is an early riser and she knows I am up in the mornings to run." Brynne looked at my mouth, her eyes darting as she read me. I wished I knew what she was thinking. What was in her heart. I'd pushed up very close to her body, but didn't touch. I just wanted to absorb the fact that I had her back in one piece.

"Don't do that again, Brynne. I'm serious. Those times of going off on your own are over."

The lift doors opened and she ducked around me to get out. I followed her down the hall and unlocked the door to my flat. As soon as we were inside she let me have it. Her eyes flared and got sparkly. She was very, very pissed, and utterly beautiful in a way that got me hard as stone. "So I'm not even allowed to go down to Java's and get a coffee?" she demanded.

"Not exactly. You are not allowed to go *alone,* and especially without telling anybody!" I shook my head in exasperation at what she'd done, threw down my keys and scrubbed my head. "Why is this concept so fucking difficult to comprehend?"

She stared at me oddly like she was trying to figure me out. "Why are you really so angry, Ethan? Going for coffee in the light of day with people all around could not have been that much of a risk." She folded her arms beneath her breasts again.

"For all I knew, you'd broken off with me again and gone home to your place!" *The truth is evil sometimes. Did I just say that out loud?*

"Ethan! I wouldn't just do that." She glared at me. "Why would you think that I would?"

"Because you've done it before!" I yelled. *There was that evil bastard truth again, worming his way into places and having a field day with my insecurities.*

"Fuck you!" she hissed, hair flying as she spun around and fled into the bedroom, slamming the door as she went in.

Fucking hell, she so needed a good shagging. I could think of a few things that would shut her up. You'd think after last night she would wake up soft and obliging like a sleepy kitten. No such luck. I had a spitting-mad feral cat on my hands.

I realized I'd left the coffee she'd bought me sitting in the drink holder down in my car. Fuck the bloody coffee, I needed a bottle of Van Gogh and about a dozen smokes.

I also needed a shower and to make a few things perfectly clear to my utterly frustrating female. Christ, she was a handful when she got like this, but a shower first and then maybe I could sit her down and attempt some logical reasoning. I went the back way to the bathroom rather than in through the bedroom because I imagined her dressing for work in there, and figured some privacy would be appreciated considering she'd just told me to sod off. I ditched my shoes and shirt and stepped in.

And had to reach for my eyeballs as they bugged out of my head and rolled around on the floor. Brynne stood there half naked in some really fucking sexy lingerie, doing her makeup or hair or something.

She twisted and gave me a look that spoke volumes about how angry she still was. "I found the note I left for you." She picked up a piece of paper from the vanity. "It was *under* the sheets where you shoved it," she smirked, let the paper fall, and then turned back to the mirror, flashing her gorgeous backside in some decadent, black lace knickers that made me feel certain my optic nerves were shot.

I thought about her arse and last night. What we'd done, and what we hadn't done . . .

Her eyes caught mine in the mirror just before she looked down, her chest flushing pink over the curves of her tits in that black lace bra I was insanely jealous of.

That's my girl.

She was remembering too. Some things between us might be fucked up right now, but in the sex department we were solid.

"We are not even close to being done discussing how the

security works in regards to you." I stepped up behind her, bringing my hand up to her hair and grabbing a handful. She inhaled deeply and flared her eyes up to mine in the mirror. "And you are in so much trouble right now." I tugged her head to the side and bared her neck so I could get at it.

"Ahhhh," she breathed heavier. "What are you doing?"

I descended on her neck and dragged my lips up the slim curve, nipping with my teeth. I bit just enough to get some sounds out of her. She smelled so good the scent intoxicated me to the point I was not going to maintain much control for long.

"Not me. You're going to be the one to say. You're going to tell me what to do, baby. What am I doing to you first?" I kept one hand in her hair and brought the other one to her flat stomach and splayed it out, pressing hard as I lowered it down beneath the fine lace.

She squirmed but I held her tight, my middle finger sliding right between her folds and over her clit. "This?" I moved my finger back and forth, lubricating her, getting her good and wet for me, but not penetrating. She would have to work for it.

"Oh, God," she moaned.

I tugged her hair a little. "Wrong answer, my beauty. You didn't tell me what I'm doing to you yet. Now say, 'Ethan, I want you to . . .'" I removed my hand from between her legs and brought the finger that'd been sliding around her quim up to my mouth. I sucked it clean with plenty of show. "Mmmmm, like spiced honey." I nipped at her neck again.

She was frustrated and hot and needy, and I was enjoying punishing her for what she'd done. She leaned into me and squirmed her arse cheeks against my cock. I pulled my hips back and laughed low at the sound of her protests when I did.

"Ethan."

I clucked at her and tugged on her hair again. "Such a defiant little thing today. I'm still waiting, baby. Tell me what you want from me." I brought my free hand down to her ass and gripped the cheek roughly. "You started this little game and you know it, so tell me what I'm going to do to you." She gasped when I dug my fingers in and tried to thrust back against my cock again. "Nope. You're not getting that until you ask nicely for it." I hauled my hand back and brought it down onto her arse with a smack. She yelped and stiffened up on her toes, arching like the beautiful goddess she was.

"Ethan, I want you . . ." She softened and tried to turn her head against my chest.

"Mmmmm, so you liked getting smacked on your gorgeous arse, yeah? Shall I give you another?" I whispered right up against her ear. "You deserved that little spanking, baby. You know you deserved it, and you still haven't done as I've asked, you naughty thing. Tell me what I'm going to do to you up against the sink."

She cried out a lovely, submissive sound that had my heart pounding and my cock about to blow.

"Tell me!" I smacked her arse again, holding my breath as I waited for her response.

"Ahhh!" She rose up in an elegant arch and opened her mouth in a gasp. I knew I'd won, I knew she'd tell me, and the thrill was like nothing I've ever known when she said the words. "Ethan, you're going to fuck me up against the sink!"

"Bend over it and hold on to the edge," I ordered, backing

off her to wait for her compliance. She trembled a bit but got into position just like I'd told her to, looking so sexed it was nearly impossible to wrap my brain around this mindfuck we were indulging in, but man it felt too good to stop.

I shoved my fingers under the elastic of that skimpy black lace and tore it down, pushing her legs apart as she stepped out. I could smell the spice of her arousal, her need for me, for what only I could give to her. I dragged the waist of my joggers open and took cock in hand. I slid it over her wet cleft and rubbed right on her clit but still without penetration. "Is this what you've been wanting, my love?"

Brynne writhed her pussy over the bell end and tried to get down on my cock. I gave her points for effort, but I was the one calling the shots and I needed more from her yet. My girl had a little more work to do before she got her reward.

I returned to her hair and took another handful, stretching her neck back elegantly. "Answer the question, baby," I said softly. Her beautiful throat moved beneath her swallowing as we looked at each other in the mirror. The hair-pulling was a trigger for her. I never jerked hard enough to hurt, just enough to maneuver her body and dominate during sex. It made her wild, and if she hadn't got off on it I would never do it. I was all about pleasing my girl.

"Yes, I want your cock, Ethan. I want you to fuck me with it and make me come! Please!" She was trembling against my body, absolutely simmering with heat.

I laughed and licked up her neck, which was stretched out for me. "Good girl. And what is the truth, baby?" I rubbed over her very sensitive clit some more and waited, loving the taste of her skin and the smell of arousal coming off her.

"The truth is ... I'm yours, Ethan! Now, please!" she begged, filling my heart to bursting at the sound of those words.

Absolute perfection. "Yes you are, and I aim to, baby. Pleasing you pleases me." I positioned the tip and impaled myself as far as I could go. We both made cries when our bodies connected.

I kept hold of that silky hair as I fucked into her so I could see her lovely eyes through the mirror. That's my thing. I don't know why, but with Brynne I need her eyes when we fuck. I want to look into them and see every sensation, every thrust and pull of our sexes grinding and gripping, driving us forward toward the end, until we lose ourselves in a feeling that can only arrive between the two of us together.

There's a truth to looking into your lover's eyes when you come, and drowning in Brynne's eyes when it happened was a thing so powerfully connective, it bound me to her in a way that meant something important and real. The intensity of what was going on between us scared me, actually. It made me extremely vulnerable, but it was too late now. I had already fallen.

Her inner muscles pulled in around me as she contracted into orgasm, crying out my name and shuddering. I kept pumping into her depths, feeling every clench and grab of her cunt as I fed her my cock. She felt so good convulsing around my shaft it made my eyes sting.

Brynne's body was made for the act of sex, but it was her that mattered. It was *her* that I loved. The seconds just before I climaxed, I thrust into her as deep and as far as I could and put my teeth down on her shoulder. She cried and I registered the sound of her, but couldn't know if it was from pain or pleasure. I didn't mean to hurt her, but I was nearly out of my mind in that instant, just wanting to hold on to her, keep her with me, fill her up with my cum, make her mine.

As the stuff spilled out of me and up into her, I told her again.

"I . . . love . . . you . . ."

I looked into her eyes, at the mirror when I said it.

We didn't make it to work anywhere close to on time. Didn't matter. Some things are more important. We were both shattered from the sex and could barely stand after, so I picked her up and took her into the shower with me. I washed her all over and let her wash me. We didn't talk. We just stared and touched and kissed and thought. After the shower I wrapped her in a towel and took her back to bed; it was only then, with her stretched out beside me all soft and content, that we spoke about things.

"It's not safe for you to go out alone. You can't anymore. We don't know the motives and I won't risk you." I spoke soft but firm; I wasn't budging on this point, and it needed to be said. "That's it."

"Really? It's that bad?" She looked surprised, and then that fearful look I'd seen before appeared on her face.

"It's not known what's going on in Oakley's camp or his opponent's. We have to assume Oakley's got his eye on you, Brynne. He knows where you've been these years, where you work, where you live, and probably your friends too. I need to have a talk with Gabrielle and Clarkson soon. They should be briefed in the event they are approached because of their connection to you. Your friends know everything, right?"

She nodded sorrowfully. "I just don't see why people would want to hurt me. I didn't do anything, and I certainly don't want to bring up the past. I just want to forget it ever happened! How is this my fault?"

I kissed her forehead and rubbed her chin with my thumb. "Nothing's your fault. We're just going to be careful with you. Very, very careful," I said, kissing her on the lips three times in succession.

"I don't want anything from Senator Oakley," she whispered.

"That's because you're not opportunistic. Most people would exploit him for money to keep it quiet. You haven't done that and they are watching to see what you might do. And I'm certain they are watching to see if Oakley's enemies try to get to you. And truthfully, his political enemies are who concern me more. The video and Oakley's knowledge of it make him culpable, bottom line. His adult son and friends committed a crime and he covered it up. Oakley's opponents would find this information a political treasure trove. Not to mention a really sordid news story to sell lots of papers."

"Oh, God." She rolled from her side to her back, throwing her arm up over her eyes.

"Hey now." I pulled her right back to facing me. "None of that, okay? I'm going to make sure they leave you alone for a lot of reasons. It's my job for one thing, and you're my girl for another." I held her face close. "That hasn't changed for you, has it?" I didn't let her go, because I needed the reassurance. I had to know. "Last night was . . . fucked up—"

"My feelings haven't changed," she interrupted. "I'm still your girl, Ethan. Last night didn't change anything with me. You have your dark place and I have mine. I understand."

I rolled her into the covers and kissed her slow and thorough, letting her know just how much I needed to hear those words. Still, I wanted more from her. Always more. How could I ever get enough when she was so sweet and beautiful and lovely?

"I'm sorry about this morning," she said, tracing my bottom lip with her finger. "I promised I wouldn't leave you like that again, and I meant it. I'm sad that you thought I would do it too. You scared me when you woke up from your nightmare, Ethan. I hated seeing you hurting like that."

I kissed her finger. "The selfish part of me was so glad you were here. Seeing you was such a relief, I cannot even express the emotions that went through me when I saw you safe beside me. But the other part of me hated what you witnessed." I shook my head. "I *hated* you seeing me like that, Brynne."

"You've seen me after a nightmare and it didn't change how you feel," she said.

"No, it didn't."

"So how is it any different for me, Ethan? And you won't share with me . . . you won't let me in." She sounded hurt again.

"I—I don't know . . . I'll try, okay? I've not spoken to anybody much about what happened. I don't know if I can . . . and I know I don't want to subject you to that dark place. It's nowhere I want you to go, Brynne."

"Oh, baby." She drew her fingers over my temple and stared into my eyes. "But I would go there for you." She searched me.

"I want to be important enough for you to tell me your secrets, and you have to let me in too. I'm a good listener. What was that dream?"

I wanted to try to be normal for her; I just didn't know if I could. I guess it was something I'd have to face up to if I wanted to keep her. Brynne was stubborn, and a part of me knew she wouldn't just let this go because I said I didn't want to talk about it.

"You are important enough, Brynne. You're all that matters."

I traced her hairline with my finger and kissed her again, sweeping deeply with my tongue, savoring her sweet taste and loving her gentle acceptance of me. But the kiss had to end eventually, and there was still my monster to face.

I pulled up some bravery from somewhere and took a deep breath, rolling away onto my back and looking up at the skylight. The day had become as gray as my mood, and it looked like rain was imminent. Right in tune with where my head was—all fogged up. Brynne stayed on her side, waiting for me to say something.

"I'm sorry for last night, and how I was with you afterward. I was overbearing and it was way too much." I spoke softer. "Forgive me?"

"Of course I do, Ethan. But I want to understand why." She reached out a hand and put it over my heart and left it there.

"That nightmare was from a time when I was in the SF. My team was ambushed, most of them killed. I was the senior officer and my weapon jammed. I got taken . . . the Afghans held me in interrogation for twenty-two days."

She inhaled sharply. "Is that how you got the scars on

your back? Did they do that to you?" Her voice was soft, but I could hear the worry in her words.

"Yeah. They shredded my back with rope beatings . . . and other things."

She gripped me a little tighter and I swallowed hard, feeling my anxiety rise. But I kept going on, feeling bad for misleading her but unable to correctly explain that my worst scars were not the ones on my back.

"I dreamed of something that—that happened . . . and it was a time when I thought I was going to be—" I stopped. My breath was coming so hard that I couldn't say any more. I just couldn't bring it up. Not to her.

"Your heart is pounding." She brought her lips down and kissed over the place where that beating muscle pumped my blood. I put my palm on the back of her head and held her there, rubbing over her hair again and again. "It's okay, Ethan, you don't have to say any more until you feel like you can. I'll be here." Her voice had that saddened tone again. "I don't want you hurting more because of me."

I stroked her cheek with the back of my finger. "Are you real?" I whispered.

She glimmered at me and nodded.

"When I woke up this morning and you were gone, I thought you might have left me because of that fucked-up situation last night and I just lost it. Brynne . . . I can't be without you now. You know that, don't you? I just cannot do it." I fingered over the red mark on her shoulder where I nipped her with my teeth when I was in the throes of that volcanic orgasm at the sink. "I marked you up. I'm so sorry 'bout that too." I ran my tongue over the mark.

She shivered against my mouth. "Listen." She took hold of my face and held me. "I love you, and I want to be with you. I know I don't say it all the time, but that doesn't mean I feel it less. Ethan, if I didn't want to be with you, or I couldn't be with you, I wouldn't be . . . and you would know it."

I exhaled with relief so great it took me a minute to find my voice. "Say that again."

"I love you, Ethan Blackstone."

Chapter 10

♣ ♠ ♥ ♦

Gladstone's for lunch and Ivan was late. I don't know why I bother trying to be punctual with my cousin, because he certainly doesn't. I checked my watch and looked around the room. Formerly a gentleman's club in the past century, the place had been reanimated with white linens, lots of glass, and light woods, looking nothing like the exclusively male societal enclave for the entitled Londoners of a hundred years ago.

Well, Ivan would certainly have fit in. My cousin was a peer of the realm even if he hated to be reminded and certainly didn't act like it. None of us can help how we are born, and Ivan couldn't control that his father had been the previous Baron Rothvale any more than I could control that my dad drove a London cab. We had connections that went far deeper than money could ever take us anyway.

Who was I kidding? Ivan could drop off a cliff if he liked, I had two beautiful women at the table looking happy and gorgeous across from me—my girl and her best friend.

"You ladies look like shopping has agreed with you." I poured for both of them from the Riesling I'd ordered.

Brynne and Gabrielle grinned and looked at each other conspiratorially, obviously sharing female secrets of a mystery I could only guess at. They'd been having a shopping excursion for dresses when I got a text from Brynne asking me what I was doing for lunch. Since they were only a few blocks over from Gladstone's I told them to add on to my luncheon date with Ivan. I wanted to introduce him to Brynne anyway, hopeful that he could wield some influence over at the National Gallery for her. Hell, I'm not too proud to ask for a favor. Not that he would give a rip. The man was on the board of one of the most prestigious art museums in the world and couldn't have cared less about it if he tried to. In fact, I am sure Ivan would resign if he could get away with it.

"It did, Ethan. Brynne got the most fabulous vintage dress for the Mallerton Gala. You just wait," Gabrielle warned me.

I made a face. "So you're saying she'll be even more lovely than normal." I looked at Brynne blushing and then back to Gabrielle. "Just what I need—more admirers chasing after her. I thought I could rely on you, Gabrielle, for just a smidge of help here?" I implored. "Why didn't you take her to a place that sells unattractive bathrobes instead?" My words were joking, but inside I was deadly serious. I hated when men looked at Brynne like they were picturing her naked.

Gabrielle shrugged. "Aunt Marie turned us on to the shop. That woman has mad skills with the unique and rare. Vintage little gem that it is, tucked away in a quiet corner of Knightsbridge. I know I'll be going back." She smirked at me. "You need the competition anyway, Ethan, it's good for you." She took a sip of her wine and turned her attention to checking messages on her mobile.

"Not true. I'm struggling enough as it is, thank you very much!" I picked up Brynne's hand and kissed it. "I'm glad you came for lunch."

She just smiled at me and said nothing in that mysterious way of hers. I wished we were alone.

Gabrielle was a devoted friend from what I could tell, and fiercely protective of Brynne. We had an understanding that was workable as long as she saw me as friend and not foe—I'd passed the test so far. Beautiful too in her own right, just not my flavor of female. Her long brown hair, with just the faintest hint of dark red glinting through, combined with very green eyes, was striking. Nice figure too; even if she wasn't my type, I still had eyes in my head and wasn't dead.

The color of her eyes reminded me of Ivan's eyes. Same green. I wondered what he would think of her when he got a look, the womanizer that he was. I bet he would like her very much. I had to stifle a laugh. Gabrielle would probably tell him to sod off to his face and he would lick his lips and ask her to join him without a hitch. Would be a riot to watch if he ever got his arse here.

Brynne's roommate was another American living in London, studying art at university, and making her way . . . away from home. Her dad was a British citizen, though. London

Met Pol—one Robert Hargreave, Chief Inspector, New Scotland Yard. I'd looked him up, and from all accounts he was solid, a respected detective on the force. I supposed I should set up a meeting with him at some point too. Although things had been very quiet on the Senator Oakley front. No news was good news . . . I hoped.

"What color is your amazing dress that will make me mad with jealousy when men drool over you wearing it?" I asked Brynne.

"It's periwinkle." She smiled again. "Aunt Marie met us there and we had so much fun with her. She really does have the eye for fashion."

"You should have brought her along for lunch with you."

"I would have loved for her to come with us, but she was off to a ladies luncheon with her book club. She said to tell you how much she's looking forward to meeting you." Brynne blushed again, as if the idea of our people meeting for the first time made her shy.

She had a shyness to her that was charming in public but didn't carry over into the bedroom with me. Nope. My girl wasn't shy with me like that, and it was *all* good. I thought about how many more hours until tonight when I could get her back into my bedroom and she could show me her un-shy side some more.

We'd been burning up the sheets lately . . . and the shower walls . . . my office desk . . . the rug in front of the fireplace . . . the balcony lounger, and even the gym. I shifted in my chair and remembered that morning *workout* with great fondness. Who knew how much fun a weight bench could be with Brynne naked and sliding up and down my—

"You'll love Marie, Ethan," Gabrielle said distractedly, still checking her messages and interrupting my erotic musings. I needed to rearrange my cock but forced a smile at both of them instead.

I had yet to meet the adored Aunt Marie but was about to very soon. We had decided it was time to bring our families together in a dinner at my place. My dad, Brynne's aunt, Gabrielle, Clarkson, Neil and Elaina made up the short list. We'd discussed it and felt it was time to get everyone on board with what was happening with us, and the possible threats to Brynne. Everyone was principal enough that they needed to know what might be in play. Brynne was too important to me to take a risk at this point, and everyone involved already knew her background anyway.

"Well I cannot wait to meet her. She sounds like she dotes on you." I checked my watch again. "I can't believe Ivan just not showing like this. So rude."

"Why don't you call him?" Brynne suggested.

"That would be a total waste of my time. He never answers his mobile. I doubt he even turns the damn thing on," I answered dryly.

"Oh, man!" Gabrielle looked up from her messages. "I'm going to have to get over to the university. Trouble with a painting. An accident involving solvent getting dumped on a rare—get this, Brynne—Abigail Wainwright." Gabrielle looked absolutely horrified, stood up abruptly and gathered her bags. "Not a good combination."

"No, that's not good at all," Brynne said, shaking her head, "the solvent will eat through the canvas if they don't neutralize."

I tried to keep up with the art geek stuff they talked about, but it wasn't easy for me. I don't think I have an artistic bone in my body. I can appreciate it, though. Brynne's portrait was the epitome of art, in my opinion.

"Do you want a ride back? Neil will take you over there if you like," I offered.

"No, that's okay. I'll get a cab—it'll be faster. I need to go right now, but thanks. I'll see you at your place tomorrow night, Ethan. Enjoy your lunch, you two."

"Let me know how it works out," Brynne told her. "If anyone can fix the mess, it's you, Gaby!"

Gabrielle hugged Brynne, waved off and left, her tall, curvy form attracting plenty of looks from appreciative males as she made her way out of Gladstone's.

I smiled at Brynne and took both of her hands. "So I get you all to myself for lunch after all." I whispered the rest. "Too bad we're in public."

"I know. We never get to do this." She squeezed my hands a little. "You've had so much work lately, and I can only imagine with the Olympics. God, that's huge, Ethan. All those people." She grinned. "William and Kate!"

I nodded. "Yes. They will be there for events. Prince Harry too. He's good fun."

"You know him?" she asked incredulously.

I nodded again. "I can try to get an introduction if you like . . . as long as you don't have a thing for princes with ginger hair."

"Never," she told me with seductive eyes. "I am partial to security guys with dark hair."

Who had turned on the blast furnace? I actually looked

around the room for an exit. If there was a door marked Private I swear I'd have had her behind it and naked in two seconds flat.

"You are so very cruel, Miss Bennett."

She looked immensely pleased with herself sitting there across from me in the restaurant. So pleased, in fact, she made me think fondly of the spanking I'd given her over the sink. God, she was a sexy thing, bent upon driving me mad.

"So back to your job. You are doing VIP security for the flippin' Olympics, Ethan!" Her excitement brought me out of my head. Probably a damn good thing right now.

"Well, I'm not complaining, it's good for business, but I could do without the stress. I just want everything to run smooth. No plots or crazies with an axe to grind for their bullshit cause, no bombs, or embarrassments, and I can breathe. Happy clients kept safe and I'll be pleased." I reached for my wine. "Let's order. I don't think Ivan's going to show . . . always bloody late for everything!" I grumbled, opening my menu.

Brynne told me what she wanted in case the waiter appeared, then excused herself for the ladies. I watched her walk away, and the looks she got from others as well. I sighed. As much as Brynne carried her reserve, she still had that certain something that made people notice her. Something I could have done without for sure but understood was part of the deal with her. Men would always look at her. *And want her. And try to take her away.*

Work was going utterly mad for me, and the busier I got, the more stretched my focus became on the job at hand and the less able I became to watch out for her safety. The past two weeks had been good for Brynne and me and our relationship, but not without worry. The worry would never go away. I've been in the security business long enough to know that when things seem most in order it's not the time to let down your guard. She was still very vulnerable, and the thought made me insane.

"Sorry, E. Lost track of the time and all that," Ivan interrupted, plopping down across from me.

"Nice of you to show up. For the appointment that *you* made, I might add. And don't sit there. Brynne's with me." I pointed to the next chair. "She'll be back in a moment."

Ivan moved to the next chair over. "Something came up and I got waylaid."

"Yeah," I snorted. "Your cock got waylaid. Who were you in bed with this time?"

"Bugger off, it wasn't that. Damn reporters dogging me—say, I need something more substantial than that." He eyeballed the wine and motioned for a waiter, the hollow look of pain showing for just an instant before he masked it away from prying eyes.

I let him be. My cousin had his faults, but then everyone has. It didn't mean he'd deserved the lot he'd gotten either. Yeah, Ivan was just as fucked up as the rest of us.

Brynne made her way back to the table a few moments later, her expression unreadable, but if I could guess, I'd say she had something on her mind. I wondered what it was.

I stood and reached for her hand, kicking Ivan's chair leg in the process so he'd get off his arse. He jumped up and widened his eyes when he saw her. I wished I'd kicked his leg instead of just the chair's leg.

"Brynne, my cousin, Ivan Everley. Ivan, Brynne Bennett, my very beautiful, and, I might add, very *taken*, girlfriend."

"*Enchanté*, Brynne." He took her hand and offered a kiss that barely passed as neutral in my book, but then did I expect anything different from him?

Stupid rhetorical question.

She smiled beautifully as always, greeting Ivan politely as I seated her and then myself. Ivan just stood there like a dimwit.

"You can sit down now. And put your tongue back in your mouth," I said.

"Well, Brynne, I was prepared to ask you how you managed to snag Ethan, but now that I've met you finally, I think the better question is for him." Ivan made a show of looking at me. "How in the hell did you capture such an exquisite creature as this, E? I mean, just look at her! And you? Well, you are so dull and surly all the time." He focused back to Brynne. "My dear, what do you see in him?" His face turned to mock interest as he rested his chin on his hand, propped up by an elbow.

"God, you are such an idiot, Ivan!"

Brynne laughed and made a comment about how determined I'd been to get her out on a date with me. "He was very persistent, Ivan. Ethan never gave up on me, and I finally went out on that date." She took a sip of wine and winked at me. "The two of you are so very different. Have you always been this close?"

"Yes." We both answered her at the same time. Ivan met my eyes and we had that communication for an instant, but then turned it off just as quickly in the next beat. That conversation was for another time. This was social.

"Close to killing him!" I smirked at Brynne. "No, seriously, I keep him alive and tolerate his many annoyances, and Ivan is dutifully grateful, isn't that right, Ivan?"

"I suppose . . . it's better than wanting me dead," he answered.

Brynne laughed. "Who wants you dead, Ivan?"

"Lots of people!" Ivan and I spoke again at the same time.

We both laughed at a bemused Brynne and then the waiter showed up to do his thing, so it was a few minutes before I was able to explain about my very eclectic cousin.

"Hmmmm, where to start?" I paused for effect. "Our mothers were sisters and we've been around each other since . . . forever. Without the blood connection I doubt we'd ever have met, though. Ivan is aristocracy, you know. In heredity and in the eyes of the World Archery Federation." Ivan scowled at me. "Brynne, you are looking at Lord Rothvale, thirteenth Baron or some rot, or *Lord Ivan*, as he's called among his sporting compatriots." I gestured with a flourish. "In the flesh."

It was Brynne's turn to look shocked. "Rothvale . . . as in the gallery where I conserve paintings?"

"Well, yeah. That's my great-great-great-grandfather it's named for, but I have no connection to the Rothvale Gallery," Ivan said.

"But you do at the National," I reminded him.

Brynne looked at me, incredulous, and then back to Ivan. "You are on the board of directors at the National Gallery, Ivan?"

He blew out a huge sigh. "Well yes, my dear, but not by choice. I've inherited the appointment and can't seem to get rid of it. My knowledge is pretty weak, I am afraid. Not like you, an expert at restoring paintings, E tells me."

"I love what I do. I'm working on the most lovely Mallerton right now." Brynne looked at me and reached for my hand. "Ethan helped me solve the mystery of the title of the book the woman in the painting was holding."

"She's really brilliant, Ivan," I concurred, brushing my thumb over her hand that I didn't want to let go of. "I just translated a little French for her."

Ivan sounded amused. "Wow, you two are really into it together. Shall I leave you to your lunch in private where you can translate more French for her?"

Brynne snatched her hand away. I glared at Ivan.

Ivan answered with a smirk. "I might have a job for someone, actually. Maybe a whole crew." He shrugged. "My estate in Ireland, Donadea, has rooms and rooms full of nineteenth-century paintings. A shitload of Mallertons too." Ivan looked up sheepishly. "Pardon my French, but I need them gone through and cataloged. I don't think they've been touched in a century." He shook his head and held his hands up. "I don't even know what's all there, just that there's a ton of it and it needs a professional's attention. It's on my list of things to do." Ivan tilted his head at Brynne and offered a look that was far too flirty than it should have been for being directed at my girlfriend. "Interested?"

No, she's definitely not interested in going to your Irish estate and cataloging your paintings while you try to finagle a way to get her into bed with you!

"Yes!" Brynne said.

"Ugh," I groaned. "Only if I come along as chaperone, and

my docket is quite full until after August." I gave him a look to let him know that Brynne would go alone to his estate in Ireland over my dead and decomposing body.

"What? You don't trust me, E? Your own blood, too." He shook his head. "So sad."

"With her? No way!" I picked up Brynne's hand again, the urge to touch her overriding the fact that I was a jealous bastard with anyone who tried to flirt with her, even my cousin.

"You know, I should introduce you to Gabrielle, my roommate—she's doing her dissertation on Mallerton. She's the one to do your job, Ivan. Gaby was just here too and had to go off. It's a pity you two didn't meet." Brynne smiled sweetly, obviously pleased with her suggestion. She tugged her hand out of mine with a little pat and then a censuring look.

"Yes!" I said, suddenly interested. "Gabrielle would be perfect for the job, Ivan." The sparks flying between the two of them would be a show I wouldn't want to miss. And hell, it was Brynne's idea, so I was completely off the hook. Anything to distract him from Brynne worked for me. "I'll introduce you to her at the Mallerton Gala. Try not to talk too much and you'll be fine," I patronized. "Just show her the paintings."

He ignored me and focused instead on charming my girlfriend. "Why, thank you, Brynne. I would love to meet your friend and have her tackle the job. You have no idea. It's the proverbial monkey on my back that needs to be on his way like decades ago . . ."

Ha! Wait until you get a load of Gabrielle and you'll be wishing for that little monkey clawing at your back!

Lunch arrived at that point and we got down to it. Ivan jabbering to Brynne about nonsense, and then to me about his security problems; before I knew it, it was time to get back.

I left Brynne with Ivan while I went to get the car pulled around front. Ivan winked at me and gave assurance he'd keep a good eye on her for me. I told him thanks for buying our lunch and gave him a warning look that left no question about just how much I needed his help. I knew my cousin was just playing with me. The poor man was probably in shock to see me like this over a girl, and I'm sure he'd have plenty to say to me about her in a private conversation. *Lovely*.

I handed the ticket to the valet and scanned the area. It was habit, just something I did when I was out. A bloke in a brown jacket leaned against the building, waiting. He had that hungry look to him and a camera around his neck. I pegged him immediately as paparazzi. They lived for shots of celebrities coming and going from establishments like Gladstone's, where anyone could show up at any time.

The valet handed off my car and I got inside to wait. I tuned on the music and got "Butterfly" by Crazy Town. Perfect song, I thought, tapping my thumb on the steering wheel while Brynne and Ivan took their damn sweet time getting outside.

I wasn't thrilled about where I was taking Brynne either. Photo shoot. If there was one thing I could change about my girl, that would be it. I absolutely loathed and despised that she got naked for the camera and that other men saw her body. It was a thing of beauty, true, but I just didn't want anyone else to see what was *mine*.

My thoughts were interrupted by the car door as Ivan opened it for Brynne, kissing her on both cheeks and making a big show of saying good-bye.

At the same time, that fucking photographer started snapping pictures! They looked like celebrities even if they weren't, and Ivan technically was. *Christ Almighty!*

Brynne looked stunning on the street talking to my cousin. How would I ever survive this, I thought. The desire for a smoke nearly had me gasping, but my vice would have to wait for the moment.

"Good-bye, Ivan! It was so lovely to meet you today, and it'll be wonderful seeing you again at the Mallerton Gala soon." Brynne got into her seat and smiled up at him.

"It was lovely to meet you too, Brynne Bennett," Ivan grinned and then bent down to speak to me. "Take care of this gorgeous girl for me, now, would you? No fits and tantrums, okay, E? You can do it." He was laughing as he shut the door.

"Well, that was fun," I said sarcastically as I pulled away from the curb.

"I like your cousin a lot, Ethan. He is a character for sure. I'm glad you introduced him. I cannot believe you knew he was on the board at the National Gallery and did not tell me!" She gave me a little punch in the shoulder, which I found incredibly hot.

"Well, sorry, I know he doesn't give a crap about the art, he's just on the board." Remembering my oath to tell her everything, I continued on, "I told him about you a while ago. I wanted to see if there can be something at the National for you. I want you to have that work visa too." I looked at her across the seat from me, so beautiful and glowing, and knew I'd do anything in order to keep her in England with me. *Even what Ivan suggested in jest on the phone?*

"Oh, Ethan." She touched my leg. "That's very sweet of you, but I will get an appointment on my own. It's something really important to me. I want to earn it by myself, not from you getting a favor from your cousin. No matter how well connected he is . . . and flirty. Jesus, that man is a flirt!"

"Don't remind me. There were a few times I wanted to strangle him during lunch."

"But it's all just an act, Ethan. You must know that about him. He respects you, and I can see the relationship you two have. Like brothers almost."

"Yeah, Ivan's good deep down. He's just had some hard knocks lately which have jaded him." *Haven't we all.*

"Haven't we all," she said.

I grabbed her hand and held it on my lap in a sort of answer. Didn't know what to say in response to that and knew we didn't have far to drive.

I dearly wished the trip could have taken a lot longer, though. The closer we got to her destination, the fouler my mood became. By the time I pulled up to the studio where she was working today and parked the damn car, I was a rabid mess. I felt irrationality sweep through my body and had to fight it off hard. My inner Mr. Hyde was having a field day with my inner Dr. Jekyll. Like kicking the good doctor's noble arse to the curb and delivering sucker punches with glee.

"What are you shooting today?" I demanded. *And please say there are* some *clothes involved.*

"Ethan," she warned. "We've been through this before. You can't come in and you need to stop worrying. It's just me and the photographer, and some time behind the camera lens. We're all professionals doing our jobs." She paused. "There is some lingerie involved."

"Which photographer?" I asked.

"Marco Carvaletti. You met him before."

"Oh, I remember the suave Italiano Mr. Carvaletti who likes to kiss you *very* well, my darling."

"You can stop being an idiot now, Ethan," she told me in no uncertain terms. "This is my job, just like you have a job."

I stared at her in the seat and wanted to tell her she couldn't go in there and take off her clothes. I wanted to stand in the back of the room and watch everything Carvaletti did, every move he made, every suggestion he directed to her. I wanted to be there in case he tried to touch her or looked too close. I wanted to turn the car around and take her home. I wanted to fuck her up against the wall the moment we got inside again. I wanted to hear her pant out my name as she was coming. I wanted her to feel *me* inside her—to know it was me there and nobody else. I wanted so much.

And I couldn't have any of those things. Nothing.

I had to kiss her good-bye and go back to *my* job. I had to tell her to text Neil when it was time for a pickup because I had an afternoon meeting and couldn't come for her. I had to watch her go and wait until the door closed behind her and she was inside the building. I had to drive away and leave my girl inside that building.

I had to do it all.

And hated every bloody second of it.

• • •

I wasn't in much of a better mood by the time I could leave the office. I rang Brynne and got voice mail. I left her a message and told her I'd bring the dinner because I knew how tired she was after a photo shoot. *Don't think about the motherfucking photo shoot.*

I wasn't worried when she didn't pick up, because I knew she was at home. Neil always checked in with me when he dropped her. I had hoped we could stay at my place tonight, but Brynne wasn't going for it. I'd asked and she'd balked. Said she needed her own bed for the night, plus she'd be over tomorrow for the family dinner we had planned. I tried to get her over with me every night, but she was still elusive about relinquishing her independence. Brynne got annoyed with me if I interfered too much or tried to influence her choices.

Cue the nude modeling. *You're thinking about it again, arsehole.*

Damn, relationships are a lot of fucking work . . . like all the goddamn time.

So, being the brilliant sod that I am, I could weigh my options—my place with no Brynne vs. the package deal of Brynne and her tiny flat, and less privacy if Gabrielle was around.

Easy decision. Brynne won every time.

Hell, I was still fantasizing about another wall-shag and wondered if I might surprise her with one if the coast was clear when I got over there.

Where to pick up food? We liked a lot of different things. I would have brought lasagna from Bellisima's, but I immediately was reminded about Carvaletti being Italian and shot that idea right down to hell. *That bastard saw her naked today.*

Brynne loved Mexican, but it was far better when she made things from scratch than any restaurant in town. I really loved the South American influences on what she liked to make. I decided on Indian and rang in an order for some butter chicken, lamb curry and veggie salad. I was just leaving the restaurant with the food when I sent off a quick text: **Almost there, baby. I got Indian chicken & lamb.**

I received something right back from her: **Hi. Really tired and just want bed. Can I skip dinner 2nite?**

What? I didn't like the sound of her message and immediately tried to figure out what she meant by it. A flicker of unease ran through me. Was she telling me not to come over, or just that she wasn't hungry? I couldn't tell from that text, and I read it over about ten times.

I was tired myself, crabby, rumpled and nicotine deprived, and not at all sure my brain was up for a conversation with a possibly irrational female mind. All I wanted was to eat something, have a shower and crawl into bed with her. I could skip the sex even, but sleeping with her was nonnegotiable.

We'd made an agreement of sorts about where we stayed, because her place or mine, I wanted her next to me. I'd made that perfectly clear to Brynne when we started out. I rang her from the car and drove.

"Hi. I'm not hungry, Ethan." She sounded odd.

"Well what's wrong, baby? You're not feeling well?" This was unusual. She'd never been sick before, except for the headache that first night we met.

"My stomach hurts. I was lying down."

"Like you're going to be sick? You want me to stop at the chemist and get you something for it?" I offered.

She paused before answering cryptically, "No, like I have cramps."

Ahhhh. The Curse. I knew about that from having a sister, I'd just never had to deal with it in a relationship before. Matter of fact, I'd never had a relationship like the one I was in with Brynne. When you have sex with short-timers, inconveniences like "she's having her dead week" don't come up. But I'd heard the complaints from friends for years, and I'd been around my sister. And I'd learned enough to know that giving a woman her space when she's hormonal is the way to go. *You think?!* I supposed the nice wall-shag I had in mind was out of the picture now too. Damn.

"Okay, I can give you a massage when I get there. Is everything else all right? How did the shoot go?" I felt myself tense up just waiting for her to answer me.

"Ummm, the shoot was fine. Good." She paused and made a sniffling sound. "I talked to my mom on the phone." She sounded sad and I wondered if the reason she sounded snuffly was because she'd been crying. Made sense. That woman almost made me feel like crying from the one time we'd spoken.

"Our conversation didn't go so great."

"I'm sorry, baby. I'll be there and we can talk when I get up to you."

"I don't want to talk about her," she snapped back. She had that lovely pissed-off tone to her voice that actually got me a bit hard, but also got my warning flaps going too.

I paused a beat. "That's fine too. I'll be there very soon."

"Why are you sighing into the phone at me?"

Christ. I'm sure I opened my mouth and just gaped like a goldfish because I had nothing to offer after that question. "I'm not."

"You just did it again!" she scolded. "If you're going to interrogate me about the photo shoot, and my mother, then maybe you shouldn't come over. I'm just not up for that tonight, Ethan."

Can you say wicked hormones changing my girl into Medusa and scaring the hell out of me?

"Not up for talking to me or not up for me at all? Because I do want to talk to you." I tried to keep my tone level but wasn't too confident I was succeeding. I was pretty fucking sure I couldn't do any better at keeping my cool, though. I did not like this fucked-up dialogue at all. It sucked.

Silence.

"Hello, Brynne? Am I coming over right now or not?"

"I don't know."

I counted to ten. "'I don't know' is your answer to me?" *What in the holy hell happened to our nice romantic lunch at Gladstone's? I want my sweet girl back!*

"You sighed at me again."

"Have me arrested. Look, I'm driving with a car full of Indian takeout and don't know where I'm going. Can you help me out, baby?"

I absolutely fucking refused to get in a row over this. She was having a shit day and hormonal—that I could deal with. It sucked if she wouldn't be in my arms tonight, but at least we weren't breaking up. Medusa might be messing with my night, but she would be out of the picture in a few days. I prayed.

"Okay, come get me then," she said firmly.

I couldn't believe my ears. "Come and get you? I thought you had to stay at your place tonight. You said earlier—"

She cut me right off, her tongue like a sharp-edged blade. "I've changed my mind. I don't want to stay here. I'll pack a bag and be ready for you in five minutes. Call me when you're at the curb and I'll be down."

"All right, chief," I said in utter bewilderment, waiting till she hung up before I sighed good and loud. I shook my head too. And even blew out a whistle. Then I drove over to get my snake-haired, sharp-tongued, unpredictable, and very per-plexing girlfriend, like the besotted sap that I very much was.

Women . . . frightening creatures.

Chapter 11

♣ ♠ ♥ ♦

That's going to be Aunt Marie! Ethan, can you let her in? I'm up to my elbows here." From the kitchen, Brynne gestured to her frantic last-minute prep for dinner.

"I've got it." I gave her an air kiss and said, "Showtime, yeah?"

She nodded back, looking beautiful, as always, in her long black skirt and purple top. The color was lovely on her, and since I now knew it was her favorite, I had to believe in my luck that first time when I sent her the purple flowers.

All in, baby.

I opened the door to a lovely woman of whom I had no expectations other than knowing she was Brynne's great-aunt. Sister to her grandmother on her mum's side. But the

person smiling at my doorstep was about as far from a grand-
motherly female as you could get. With her unlined skin and
dark red hair, she looked young and stylish and rather . . . hot
for a woman who could not be above fifty-five.

"You must be Ethan that I'm hearing so much about," she
said in a native tongue.

"And you must be Brynne's aunt Marie?" I hesitated in
case I was wrong, but really, the women in her family were
stunning. I wondered again what kind of beauty Brynne's
mother must be.

She laughed charmingly. "You sound a little unsure there."

I ushered her in and closed the door. "Not at all. I was expecting her great-aunt, you see, not her older sister. She's got
her hands full in the kitchen and sent me to greet you." I held
out my hand. "Ethan Blackstone. It is my very great pleasure,
Aunt Marie. I hear Brynne sing your praises all the time and
have looked forward to meeting you."

"Oh, please call me Marie," she said, taking my hand.
"Quite the charmer you are, Ethan. Her sister, hmmmm?"

I laughed and shrugged. "Too flattering? I don't think so,
and welcome, Marie. I appreciate you taking the time to join
us tonight."

"Thank you for the invitation to your lovely home. I don't
get to see my niece often enough, so this is bonus. And your
comment was lovely even if it was far too flattering. You've
got my vote, Ethan." She winked at me and I think I fell in love
with her right then and there.

Brynne came out of the kitchen and embraced her aunt.
I got a very happy grin from Brynne over Marie's shoulder. It
was clear that whatever problems she had with her mum, she

didn't have them with Marie, and that made me very glad. Everybody needs someone to give them unconditional love.

They went off to the kitchen and I went to get drinks sorted before the bell rang again. I smirked to myself at what Dad would think of Marie when he got a look at her. I knew she was a widow with no children, but with her beauty, there must be a long queue of men clamoring for her time. I couldn't wait to get the story from Brynne.

Clarkson and Gabrielle arrived next, and since they were already in good with Marie, all I had to do was make drinks and pass them around. Clarkson and I had an easy truce of sorts, along the same lines as my relationship with Gabrielle. We all cared about Brynne and wanted her to be happy. I didn't thrill about him taking her pictures, but then we were only able to be friendly because he was gay. Seriously, I know it's my issue, but if he was straight and taking nude pictures of Brynne? He wouldn't be in my home right now.

Once Neil and Elaina showed up, I felt a little more at ease in my own house. Clarkson went in to help Brynne and Marie in the kitchen while Gabrielle and Elaina seemed to hit it off by talking books—something trending about a very young billionaire and his obsession with an even younger woman . . . and sex. Lots of erotic sex scenes in the book, like apparently on every page.

Neil and I looked sympathetically at each other and had absolutely nothing to add to the conversation. I mean, who reads this crap? Who has time? Why even read about sex in a book when you can have it instead? I don't get that. And billionaires in their twenties? I mentally shook my head and pretended to care. I'm such a bastard.

I looked at my watch, and just like a summons, the bell rang. My dad, finally. I leapt out of my seat to get the door. Poor Neil looked like he wished he could come with me.

"Dad. I was getting worried. Come in and meet my girl, why don't you."

"Son." He clapped me on the back in our standard greeting and grinned. "You look happier than the last time I laid eyes on you. Hannah tells me you're going up to Somerset to visit. Taking Brynne along."

"Yeah. I want them all to know one another. Speaking of meeting, come on, Dad, she's this way." I led him into the kitchen and was greeted by the most glowing radiance on Brynne's face as she got a gander at my dad. It made my heart jump. This was important stuff. Meeting the family and making impressions. Wanting them to get on was suddenly very important to me.

"Now, this must be the lovely Brynne and her . . . older sister?" Dad said to Brynne and Marie.

"Hey! You stole my line, Dad!"

"He's right," Marie said. "Your son used the same one on me when I arrived."

"Like father, like son," Dad said, grinning happily between Brynne, Marie, and Clarkson.

"My father, Jonathan Blackstone." I jolted out of my stupor to make the introductions and rubbed my hand slowly up and down Brynne's back. I wondered how she was taking in all this. We had come so far, so fast, it was more than a little mad, but like I'd said before, there was no changing our path now. We were speeding down a mountain and weren't stopping for anything. She leaned in to my side and I gave her a little squeeze.

My dad took Brynne's hand and kissed it, just like he'd been greeting females my whole life. He told her how lovely it was to finally meet the woman who had captured me, and how beautiful she was. She blushed and introduced Marie and Clarkson. Damn if the old flirt didn't kiss Marie's hand as well. I shook my head, knowing he'd make the rounds to every woman here tonight. If they had a hand, he'd have his lips on it. Oh and yeah, he thought Marie was hot. Easy thing to spot, and I was sure.

"I won't kiss your hand, though," Dad said to Clarkson as they shook.

"If you really want to you may," Clarkson offered, in the ultimate icebreaker.

"Thanks for that, mate. I think you've stunned him speechless," I said to Clarkson.

Brynne looked at me and then at Dad. "I know where Ethan learned to do that hand-kissing thing I love so much, Mr. Blackstone. I can see he's been trained by a master," she told him with a beautiful smile. A smile with the power to light up a room.

"Please call me Jonathan, and bear with me a little more, my dear, as I take a further liberty." Dad leaned in and kissed her on the cheek! She blushed some more and got a little shy, but still she looked happy. I kept caressing up her back and really hoped it wasn't all too much of everything.

"Easy there, old man," I said, shaking my head. "My girl. Mine." I drew her very close to me until she squeaked.

"I think they get it, Ethan," she said, pressing her hand up on my chest.

"Okay, as long as nobody forgets."

"Kinda impossible for that to happen, baby."

She called me baby. It's all good now, I thought, glad I could laugh at myself as we all got down to the purpose of coming together for the evening.

"Chicken Marsala, mmmm. Brynne darling, what is that in here?" Dad asked between bites. "It's really wonderful."

"I used a chocolate wine to sauté the chicken."

"Interesting. I love what it does to the taste." Dad winked at Brynne. "So you're a gourmet?"

"Thank you, but not really a gourmet. I enjoy it and learned to cook for my dad when my parents split. I have these marvelous cookbooks by Rhonda Plumhoff on my e-reader. She links her recipes to popular books. She's famous from where I'm from. I just adore her recipes."

He tilted his head at me. "Smart son I raised."

"I'm not an idiot, Dad, and she can cook, but I had no idea about that part in the beginning. Her first meal with me was a PowerBar, so imagine my surprise when she started slinging pots and waving sharp knives in my kitchen. I just kept back and got the hell out of the way!"

"Again, you were always a quick lad," Dad said with a wink.

Everybody laughed and seemed very at ease with each other, which helped me, but I was still nervous about what I needed to tell them. Not for the security part—that I knew how to do, and very well too; it was sharing the information with Brynne present that rattled me. I didn't want to objectify her as a security job when she was so much more to me. I also didn't want to get her all tangled up in the emotionality of the situation and have her upset, and in turn have that disturb our relationship again. I was protective of us. I was protective of her. Yes I was, with no apologies to the fact, nor would my feelings change on that front. I couldn't bear to hurt her anymore with that sordid mess and wouldn't let anyone else do it either.

So we made a deal. I would brief Clarkson and Gabrielle together in my office while Brynne played hostess with the others, and then switch to Marie and my dad. That way Brynne didn't have to be in there feeling uncomfortable watching the PowerPoint I'd made with time lines and photos so everyone knew faces and names. It was important for the people closest to Brynne to know all the details of who, what, where, and the possible motivations of what may come. You couldn't get any higher political motives than a presidential election in the U.S. And the side wanting to exploit Brynne would work just as hard as the side who wanted her existence unknown. I didn't know how else to protect her and get the information out to the people that mattered. Elaina and Neil were already up to speed, and Brynne said she was comfortable with them and my dad knowing. The others already knew her history, of course.

We had a session scheduled with Dr. Roswell to go over some things as a couple. I agreed to it when she asked me. Brynne still had this idea in her head that I couldn't really love her enough to overlook where she'd been when those guys attacked and videotaped her. Like her time stamp branded her forever a whore at seventeen. It made me really sad she blamed herself. It was definitely an issue for her, not for me, but getting her to believe that I didn't love her any less because of that foul assault she'd endured was the real hurdle. We had our stuff to work on and hadn't even scratched the surface of my demons at all. And for more than the first time I wondered if I needed to talk to someone about my bits and pieces. The thought of another nightmare scared the everliving shit out of me. More so that Brynne would see me like that again.

I watched her carefully the whole night. Outwardly she looked beautiful and charming, but inside I guessed she was struggling as the evening progressed. The minute I was done with Dad and Marie I went right over to find her in the kitchen, where she was getting coffee and dessert ready for our guests. She kept her head down even though she knew I was there. I wrapped my arms around her from behind and rested my chin on top of her head. She was soft against me and her hair smelled like flowers.

"What have we here, my darling?"

"Brownies with vanilla ice cream. The best dessert on the planet." Her voice was flat.

"It looks decadent. Almost as delicious as you look to-night."

She made a sound and then she got quiet. I saw her wipe at her eye and then I knew. I turned her and took her face in my hands. I hated when she cried. Not really the tears, but the sadness behind them. "Your dad—" She couldn't finish, but she'd said enough. I pulled her against my chest and drew her further into the kitchen so people couldn't see us, and I just held her for a minute.

"You're worried what he thinks?"

She nodded against me.

"He adores you, just like everyone else does. My dad is not a judgmental fellow. It's not his way. He's just happy to

see me happy. And he knows what makes me happy is you."
I put my hands on each side of her face again. "You make me happy, baby."

She looked up at me through sad, beautiful eyes that sparkled and brightened as she comprehended my words. "I love you," she whispered.

"See?" I poked at my chest with a finger. "Very happy guy."

She kissed me on the lips and made my heart thud hard inside.

"Dessert," she said, motioning toward the counter. "The ice cream is going to melt."

It's a good thing she remembered, because I sure wouldn't have. "Let me help you with that," I said. "The sooner we serve them, the sooner they can go home, yeah?" I started picking up dessert plates and moving them out to people. If nothing else, I am a man of action.

I woke up to a whole lot of noise and fitful movement next to me. Brynne was having a dream. As in, not a nightmare, but a *dream*. At least it sure looked like it to me. She was writhing all over the place and scissoring her legs. Grabbing at her T-shirt and arching her body. She must be having a really *nice* fucking dream. And it better be me she's fucking in her dream!

"Baby." I put a hand on her shoulder and shook a little. "You're dreaming . . . don't be scared. It's just me."

Her eyes flew open and she sat up immediately, looking around the room until her gaze fixated on me. God, she was wildly beautiful with her hair all down her shoulders and her chest heaving. "Ethan?" She reached out a hand.

"I'm right here, baby." I took her hand in one of mine. "Were you dreaming?"

"Yeah, it was weird." She left the bed and went into the loo. I heard water running and a glass being set down on the counter. I waited in bed for her to come back, and after a couple minutes she did.

Boy. Did. She.

She slinked out stark naked with a look in her eyes that I'd seen before. A look that says, *I want sex and I want it NOW.*

"Brynne? What's going on?"

"I think you know," she said in a sultry voice as she climbed on top of me and looked down, her hair falling forward like a pleasure goddess intent upon ravaging me.

Oh, fuck yes!

My hands went up to her breasts without a thought. God! I cupped all that soft flesh in my hands and drew it toward my mouth. She arched and began grinding over my cock, which was now as wide awake as my brain. I forgot about her being out of commission because she sure wasn't acting like she was out of commission.

I got my mouth over her nipple and sucked it in deep. I loved the taste of her skin and could play for ages before I was ready to give her beautiful tits up. I took the other nipple and bit down a little, wanting to take her to that edge where a little pain made the pleasure so much better. She cried out and pushed harder against my mouth.

I felt her hand slip under the shorts I'd worn to bed and wrap around my cock.

"I want this, Ethan."

She hopped off my hips and her nipple left my mouth with

a pop. I didn't have time to protest the loss before she went to work on removing those annoying shorts and getting her lips down around the bell end of my cock. "Ahhh, God!" I threw my head back and let her go to work on me. It was so fucking fine, my balls ached. She was really good at this. I got a handful of her hair and held her head while she sucked me to the brink of orgasm. I so wished I could go off inside her instead of her mouth. I preferred to be up in her deep when I came, with my eyes locked onto hers.

Well, my girl had more surprises in store for me, because she said, "I want you inside me when you come."

How in the hell did she just do that?

"Is it okay?" I managed to gasp out as she moved up to leverage herself.

"Umm-hmm," she moaned, pushing up on her knees to straddle me and back down to swallow my cock all the way to my balls.

I don't know how it didn't hurt her. Maybe it did, but it wasn't me doing it, it was her taking what she most obviously wanted. *If you insist!*

"Ohhhh, fuuuuck!" I yelled, latching onto her hips and helping her out.

Brynne went wild, riding me hard, rubbing her sex where it did her the most good. The pounding rhythm exploded between us, and what was coming I knew would be huge. I felt the tightening start but desperately needed to bring her with me. There was no way I was coming without her at least joining me in the fun. I didn't operate like that.

I felt her inner core squeezing me tight and hot as she

worked herself up and down. I snaked a hand down between her legs to meet where our bodies joined and found her clit through all that wet and slippery. I wished it was my tongue, but I made do with my fingers and started stroking.

"I'm coming," she panted.

She'd said it like that before, so soft and delicate. Those two words. It made me crazed to hear it from her again. It did because it was me making her fly apart, and she gave up everything to me in the instant when it happened.

Her soft words also sent me tumbling over the edge.

"Yes you are, baby. Come. Now. Come all over me!"

I watched her go and follow my command like an expert. She squeezed and cried and gripped and shuddered.

"Ohhhhhh, Ethaaaaan! Yes. Yes. Yes!"

Coming on command. That's my girl, who does it when I tell her to. I'm such a lucky, lucky bastard.

I loved every part of watching her. Of feeling her pleasure. And when I felt myself start to go off, I slammed her down one final time while I thrust up in her as far as I could get and let it fly.

The hot flood of sperm jetted out and into her depths. I felt every spurt in sharp bursts and rode the wave of pleasure in a fucking daze, barely conscious of where my hands were gripping anymore or of what my body was doing. I got to look into her beautiful eyes, though.

Some time later—I have no idea how long—she stirred on my chest and lifted her head. Her eyes glowed in the dark and she smiled at me.

"What *was* that?"

"A really awesome middle-of-the-night shag?" she quipped.

I chuckled. "A really fucking amazing middle-of-the-night shag."

I kissed her lips and held her head until I was ready to let her go. I'm possessive like that after we have sex. I don't like to leave right away, and since she was on top of me, I didn't have to worry about crushing her and could stay a bit longer.

I thrust up deep again and made her moan a luxurious sound against my lips.

"You want more?" she asked in a voice mixed with content and surprise.

"Only if you do," I said. "I'll never turn you down, and I like it when you jump me, but I thought you were having your period—"

"No. Not like that for me because of the pills I take. It's barely anything, a day maybe, if that . . . sometimes I don't even have one." She started kissing over my chest and grazed a nipple with her teeth.

Christ, it felt so good. Her attentions jolted me right back into the moment and a healthy desire for round two.

"I think you're going to kill me, woman . . . in a really nice fucking way," I managed to say, but it was the last thing either of us spoke for a while. My Medusa had just turned into Aphrodite worshipping at the altar of Eros. My luck apparently knew no bounds.

"The U.S. papers," Frances said, setting the stack on my desk. "There's an interesting article in the *Los Angeles Times* on members of Congress with children in active military service. Guess who they interviewed?"

"He must be one of the very few. Oakley will milk it for everything he can. Thanks for these." I tapped the stack of papers. "What about the other thing?"

Frances looked very pleased with herself. "Picking it up when I go out to get lunch. Mr. Morris said it restored beautifully after so many years in the vault."

"Thank you for seeing to that for me." Frances was a gem of an assistant. She ran my company office like a tight ship. I might organize the security, but that woman kept my business sorted, and I didn't underestimate her worth for an instant.

"She's going to love it." Frances hesitated at the door. "And did you still want me to clear your schedule for Monday?"

"Yes, please. The Mallerton thing tonight and then we leave in the morning for Somerset. We'll drive back Monday evening."

"I'll see to it. Should be no problem."

As Frances left I picked up the *Los Angeles Times* and turned to the article about the senator. I wanted to be sick. The slippery serpent failed to mention how his precious son was stop-lossed just recently, but that was no surprise. I wondered what the son really thought of the father. I could only imagine the dysfunction in that family, and it wasn't a bit nice.

I set the paper back on the stack, and as I did, the movement caused something to peek out below it. An envelope. The thing had been set between the stack of papers. That in itself was odd, but the words on the envelope—FOR YOUR CONSIDERATION—and the fact that it had my name underneath got my heart pounding.

"Frances, who handed you the U.S. papers this morning?" I bellowed on intercom.

"Muriel has them ready every morning. She sets them aside like she's been doing for the last month. They were just there waiting for me." She hesitated. "Is everything all right?"

"Yeah. Thanks."

My heart was still pounding as I stared at the envelope on my desk. Did I want to look? I reached for the flap and unwound the red string tie. I stuck my hand in and pulled out photos. Eight-by-ten black-and-white photographs of Ivan and Brynne chatting at Gladstone's. Him kissing her on the cheeks as I waited for her to get in the car. Ivan leaning in to speak to me and waving us off. Ivan on the street after we'd pulled away. Ivan waiting on the street for his own car to come round.

That photographer I'd seen outside the restaurant was there specifically for Ivan? He'd gotten death threats before . . . and now we had pictures of him and Brynne and me together? Not a good connection for her. Ivan had his own shit storm of troubles, and I sure as hell didn't need the added complication of whoever was harassing Ivan dragging my Brynne into his whole mess. Fuck!

I flipped over the pictures one by one. Nothing. Until the last one. *Never attempt to murder a man who is committing suicide.*

I'd seen this kind of thing throughout my career. It had to be taken seriously, of course, but more often than not, it was some lunatic fringe who had an axe to grind on the back of someone notable they perceived to have caused offense to them personally and with cruel intent. Sports figures, especially, suffered this kind of crap. Ivan had offended a ton of people in his time and had the gold medals to prove it. A former Olympic archer now retired from the sport, he was still Britain's lauded golden boy hounded by the media. The fact he was my blood family would have earned him the protection regardless, but he certainly kept me busy.

These photos had been taken two weeks ago. Was that photographer there for Ivan specifically, or did he just sell the pictures he'd taken of Ivan Everley, Olympic archer, because he'd been lucky to snap them and could get a few pounds for selling? Paparazzi hung around places that got a lot of celebrity traffic by habit, so it was hard to tell if the pictures had been prearranged or mere chance.

And if you were a lunatic intent upon killing somebody famous, why in the hell would you bother to inform his private security detail that you were planning to do it? Made no sense at all. Why send them to me? Whoever had got the pictures obviously wanted me to see them. They'd gone to the trouble of planting them in a stack of newspapers I regularly ordered from the street cart.

Muriel.

I made a mental note to speak to Muriel on my way out. I'd be leaving early anyway because of the Mallerton thing, so I should be able to catch her before she closed up shop for the night.

I opened my desk drawer and pulled out cigarettes and my lighter. I saw Brynne's old mobile in there and pulled it out too. Not much traffic on it for the past two weeks, as all her contacts were onto her new number now. The bloke from the *Washington Review* had never rung back, most likely figuring her a bum lead, which worked perfectly in Brynne's favor. I set it up to charge so it would be ready to take with me tonight and into the weekend.

I lit up my first Djarum of the day. The inhale was perfect. I felt like I was doing fairly well with the cutting back. Brynne helped motivate me, but when things were rocky with us, it was chain-smoking central. Maybe I should try the nicotine patch thing.

I resolved to enjoy my one smoke and thought about the upcoming weekend. Our first trip together. I'd managed to scrape out three days of time so I could take my girl up to the Somerset coast to stay at my sister's country home. The place also operated as a high-end bed-and-breakfast, and I was well aware of the fact I'd never asked my sister if I could bring a guest along with me on any other occasion that I'd ever gone there before.

Brynne was different for so many reasons, and if I wasn't quite ready to own up to those feelings publically, I did recognize them for what they were. I wanted to talk to her about where we were heading, and ask her what she wanted. The only reason I hadn't already was because her potential answer made me really fucking nervous. What if she didn't want what I wanted? What if I was just her first real relationship that she could test the waters with? What if she met somebody else down the line?

My list could go on and on. I just had to keep reminding myself that Brynne was a very honest person and when she told me how she felt about me, then, well, it was the truth. My girl was no liar. *She told you she loves you.*

The plan was to leave early in the morning after the night's gala to avoid traffic, and I couldn't wait to get Brynne up there. I wanted some romantic time away with my girl, and also just needed to get out of the city and into the fresh air of the country. I loved London, but even so, the desire to have time away from the urban crush in order to keep my sanity played out regularly.

A call came through just then, pulling me out of my wool-gathering moment and back into the very demanding and very urgent present situation of my job responsibilities. The day flew, and before I knew it, it was time to get moving.

I called Brynne as I was leaving the office to tell her I was on my way. I expected to get a breathless rundown of everything that needed to be done before the thing tonight and our impending trip. I got voice mail instead. So I sent her a short text: **On my way home. Need anything?** And got no response.

I didn't like it and realized right then and there that I would always worry about her. The worry would never go away. I'd heard people say such things about their children. That they didn't know what real worry was until they had someone in their lives important enough to measure the true essence of what it meant to love another person. With that love came the burden of potential loss—a prospect too uncomfortable for me to think much about.

Remembering the envelope from the stack of newspapers, I headed over to Muriel's newsstand on my way out to my car. She saw me approaching and tracked me with her soulful eyes. She might have had a hard life and rough existence, but those truths didn't alter the fact she was very intelligent. Her sharp eyes missed nothing.

"Hello, Muriel."

"'Ello, guv. What canna do for ye? I've every American rag just like ye want, eh?"

"Yes. Very good." I smiled at her. "Question, though, Muriel." I observed her body language as I spoke, searching for clues to see if she knew what I was asking or not. I pulled out the envelope with the photos of Ivan and held it up. "What do you know about this being placed inside the stack of papers from today?"

"Nothin'." She didn't look to the left. She didn't lose eye contact either. Those two things were supportive of her giving me the truth. I could only guess and use my intuition, and remember who I was dealing with.

I set a tenner on the counter. "I need your help, Muriel. If you see anyone or anything suspicious, I want you to tell me about it. It's important. A person's life could be at stake." I gave her a nod. "Will you keep an eye out?"

She looked down at the ten-pound note and then back up to me. She flashed those horrific teeth in a genuine smile and said, "For ye, handsome, I will." Muriel snatched up the ten pounds and put it in her pocket.

"Ethan Blackstone, forty-fourth floor," I said, pointing to my building.

"I know yer name an I'll no forget."

I guessed we had as good a deal as was possible considering who I was making it with. I headed to my car, eager to get home and see my girl.

I dialed Brynne a second time and once again got voice mail, so I left a message saying I was on my way. I wondered what she was doing not to answer and tried to imagine something like taking a bath, working out with headphones in, or having her phone set to silent.

I struggled with my worries. Foremost, the emotion was still unfamiliar, but at the same time not something I could set aside either. I worried about Brynne constantly. And just because this was all new to me sure as hell didn't make it any easier to understand. I was a total novice learning my way.

The flat was silent as the grave when I stepped in. I felt my anxiety spike to very unpleasant levels and started searching. "Brynne?"

Only more silence. She wasn't working out and she definitely wasn't in my office. Not outside on the balcony. The bathroom was my last hope. My heart pounded in my chest as I opened the door. And crashed when she wasn't in there either.

Fuck! Brynne, where are you?

Her beautiful dress was hanging on a hook, though. The periwinkle one she'd bought in the vintage shop with Gabrielle on the day we met for lunch at Gladstone's. There was evidence of packing too—cosmetics out and a small bag halfway done. So she had been here getting ready for tonight and our weekend away.

I wanted to give her the benefit of the doubt, but she'd gone off alone before, and what if she had again? After those lunatic photos from today, my stomach was in knots, and I just needed to know where in the fuck she was!

I went through to the bedroom, connecting a call to Neil in my half-panicked state when I saw the most wonderful vision in the world. Amid all the scattering of clothes and half-packed bags was Brynne, curled up in the bed . . . asleep.

"Yeah?" Neil answered. I was so frozen that I still had the mobile up at my ear.

"Umm, false alarm. Sorry. We'll see you at the National in a few hours." I hung up before he could respond. Poor mate must think I've lost it.

You have *utterly lost it!*

Moving very quietly, I shrugged out of my jacket, ditched my shoes, crawled carefully onto the bed and curled around her sleeping form. I breathed in her lovely fragrance and let my heart rate slow down. The urge to light up a cig was intense but I focused on her warmth against me instead and figured my addiction to the smokes would have to lessen eventually.

Brynne was out cold, sleeping very deeply. I wondered why she was so tired but didn't want to disturb her either. I could do the watch and wait just fine with her next to me and thought about the lesson I'd just learned. Brynne wasn't the only one with trust issues, apparently. I needed to work on mine a bit more. When she said she wouldn't take off alone on me, then I had to trust she'd keep her word.

I opened my eyes to find hers studying me. She smiled, looking happy and gorgeous and a tad smug. "I like watching you sleep."

"What time is it?" I looked up at the skylight to see that daylight was still clinging. "I slept? I came home and found you in bed and couldn't resist joining you. I guess I drifted off as well, sleepyhead."

"It's about five-thirty and time to get moving." She

stretched like a cat, gloriously sensual and erotic as she un-curled. "I don't know why I was so tired. I just laid down for a minute and when I opened my eyes, you were here." She started to roll off the bed.

I latched onto her shoulder and rolled her back, pinning her underneath me and settling between her legs. "Not so fast, my beauty. I need a little alone time first. It's going to be a long night, and I'll have to share you with myriads of idiots."

She reached up, held my face and grinned. "What kind of alone time were you envisioning?"

I kissed her slowly and thoroughly, roaming my tongue over every inch of her mouth before I answered. "The kind where you are naked and shouting my name." I thrust my hips slowly into her soft body. "This kind."

"Mmmmm, you are convincing, Mr. Blackstone," she said, still holding my face, "but we do need to start getting ready for this thing tonight. How good are you at multitasking?"

"I am good at many things," I responded before I kissed her again. "Give me a hint."

"Well I do love your grotto shower almost as much as your bathtub," she said coyly.

"Ahhh, so you're just using me for my excellent bathroom amenities, then?"

She giggled and moved her hand down between us to grip my hardening cock. "Excellent amenities all the way around as I see it."

I laughed and groaned at the same time, sweeping off her and into the bathroom. "I'll get the hot water started . . . and I'll be waiting for you in there."

I didn't have long to wait before she joined me, naked and mind-bendingly sexy as usual, rendering me utterly captive and raging to claim her body with the dominating sex I couldn't seem to control when we were together. My ultimate reward and my greatest fear all rolled into one. I'd joked about the gala tonight and sharing her with others, but the statement held far more truth than I wanted to admit. I loathed sharing her with other men who admired her—far too much in my opinion.

But it was the reality of Brynne, and if she was my girl, then I'd have to learn to take it like a man.

We made very good use of the time in that hot soapy water, though. Yes, multitasking is one of my strong points, and I won't blow any opportunities I'm offered.

"You look beyond gorgeous, you know."

She blushed into the mirror, the darkening flush moving down her neck and even over the swell of her breasts in the dip of that decadent dress she'd found. It was lace and very fitted to her shape, the short skirt rather frothy of some other material I didn't know the name of. Didn't matter what the hell it was, that dress was going to be the death of me tonight. I was so fucked.

"You look pretty gorgeous yourself, Ethan. We match too. Did you pick that tie just because of my dress?"

"Of course. I have heaps of ties." I watched her doing her makeup and finishing the last bits and pieces, grateful that she didn't mind me lurking, and getting nervous for what I was about to do.

"Will you wear that vintage silver tie clip? The one I like so much?"

Perfect lead-in. "Sure." I went to my case atop the dresser to get it.

"Was it a family piece?" she asked as I pinned it onto my tie.

"Actually, it was. My mother's family. My grandparents were old English money and had only the two daughters—my mum and Ivan's mum. When they passed, the goods went between the grandkids, Hannah, me, and Ivan."

"Well, it's incredible and I love antique pieces like that. Vintage things are so well crafted, and if it has some sentimental meaning, then all the better, right?"

"I don't have but a few memories of my mum, I was so young when she died. I remember my grandmother, though. She had us stay for holidays, told us lots of stories and showed us photographs; she tried to help us know our mother as best she could because she always said it's what my mum would have wanted."

Brynne put down her makeup brush and came over to me. She drew her hand up my sleeve and then adjusted my tie a bit, and finally smoothed down over the silver clip reverently. "Your grandmother sounds like a lovely woman and so does your mother."

"Both would have loved meeting you." I kissed her carefully so as not to smudge her lipstick and pulled the box from my pocket. "I have something for you. It's special . . . meant for you." I held it out to her.

Her eyes widened at the black velvet box, and then she looked up, a little startled. "What is it?"

"Just a gift for my girl. I want you to have it."

Her hands shook as she opened the case, then one came up to her mouth in a soft gasp. "Oh, Ethan, it's—it's so beautiful—"

"It's a small vintage piece from my mother and it's perfect for you and how I feel about you."

"But you shouldn't give this family piece to me." She shook her head. "It's not right for—for you to give that away—"

"I should give it to you and I am giving it," I spoke over her firmly. "May I put it on you?"

She looked back at the pendant and then back at me, and repeated her actions.

"I want you to wear it tonight and accept the gift."

"Oh, Ethan." Her bottom lip quivered. "Why this?"

Honestly? The amethyst heart pendant with diamonds and pearls was a very pretty little thing, but more than that, it screamed Brynne's name. When I'd remembered it was in the collection of my portion of the lot from my mother's estate, I'd gone down to the vault and opened it up. There were other things in there as well, but maybe some more time was needed first before we delved any deeper with additional jewelry gifts.

"It's just a necklace, Brynne. Something very fine that reminds me of you. It's vintage and it's your favorite color and it's a heart." I took the box from her hand and removed the pendant. "I hope you'll accept it and wear it and know that I love you. That's all." I tilted my head and held the two ends of the chain in my fingers, waiting for her to agree.

She pursed her lips together, took a deep breath and got that sparkly look in her eyes as she looked up at me. "You're going to make me cry, Ethan. That's so—so beautiful and I love it—and—and I love that you want me to have it—and I love you too." She turned back toward the mirror and lifted her hair off her neck.

Victory felt so fucking wonderful! I am sure I was beaming, knowing more happiness in this moment than I'd felt in ages when clasping that chain around her beautiful neck, watching the bejeweled heart settle onto her skin, finding a home at last, after decades in the dark.

A lot like my heart.

Chapter 12

The National Portrait Gallery is a magnificent venue for events and one I am well acquainted with, having been there many times before: working security, sometimes as a guest, and once or twice with a date.

But never like this.

Brynne brought a whole new meaning to the idea of possessiveness. At least for me she did. I thought I might be dead by the end of the night from keeping up with all the people who wanted a piece of her.

She looked so beautiful and perfect in her periwinkle lace dress and silvery shoes; every inch the model she was outwardly, but inwardly, that artistic mind of hers was brilliant and respected for the work she did in her field. My girl was a celebrity tonight. It damn well helped to see my gift around her neck too. *She is mine, people! Mine! And don't fucking forget it either!*

The display of Lady Percival was indeed a hit. She'd been set up as a tutorial on the conserving process, as her restoration was only partially complete. And Brynne, of course, was credited as conservator for the project. As we went in to be seated for dinner, mention was made of her discovery in the welcome speech. The look of pride on her face was something I don't think I'll ever forget. All of the proceeds for the night's event went to support the Rothvale Foundation for Advancement of the Arts, and as I looked around the room, I could see big money and old names among the guests. It seemed that Mallerton was experiencing a renaissance of sorts, and Brynne's disclosure of what he'd painted had helped generate interest in his work and, as a result, the Rothvale charity.

"Brynne, your Lady Percival is something else," Gabrielle said. "I got a good look at her when I arrived. I love how they are displaying her as an opportunity for teaching about the conserving methods and process that go into a treasure like her. And, Ethan, you were instrumental in solving the mystery too, I hear."

"Hardly instrumental. Just some word translation, but thank you, Gabrielle. I was glad to help my girl with a little French." I winked at Brynne. "She looked so happy when she figured it all out."

"I was ecstatic. That painting was a career-maker for me. And I owe it all to you, baby." She reached over and covered my hand with hers.

God, I loved when she made little gestures of affection

like that. I brought her hand to my lips and didn't care one bit who saw. I just didn't care.

"I wonder where Ivan is. Do you think he'll be here soon?" Brynne asked me.

My feelings of joy turned to pure jealousy in about two point five seconds, and I am sure I frowned before I caught myself and accepted she was just being nice. I was reminded that I needed to let him know about the pictures from today, but damn, Ivan would drool all over Brynne when he saw how beautiful she looked tonight.

Brynne turned to her friend and started in excitedly, "Gab, I really hope he comes tonight, I so want you to meet Ethan's cousin. He has a houseful of Mallertons that need cataloging and God knows what else. You *need* to meet this man. I mean, you really need to."

Gabrielle laughed, looking very happy and lovely in her own right, wearing a fitted green dress that did wonderful things paired with her coloring and matching green eyes. This could be a very good fixation, I realized. An Ivan distracted by Gabrielle would be excellent for keeping him from flirting with Brynne. And something told me Ivan was going to be all over Gabrielle once he got a good look at her. I'd wager brass on it. And I'd win too.

"Hard to say, baby. Ivan sees time in his own set of parameters and he always has. It's terribly annoying . . ." My words trailed off when I saw her across the table. *Bugger me.* Strawberry Blonde at three o'clock—all decked out and on the hunt. *Not good.*

I glanced away quickly and focused on Brynne. She looked over to where my eyes had just been and then back at me.

Her mind was going in circles, I am sure. Brynne's a smart girl. I tried to play it cool and prayed that Pamela or Penelope did not remember any better than I did, but I didn't hold out much hope. She was a friend of Ivan's and I just knew she would end up approaching me before the night was through. Where is the rule book for handling these awkward situations? Wasn't it just plain vulgar to introduce the last person you'd shagged to the person you were shagging now? Bleh.

"Is everything okay?" Brynne asked.

"Yes." I reached for my wineglass and put my arm on the back of Brynne's chair. "Perfect." I smiled.

"Oh, look, there's Paul." She grinned and waved at my enemy, who raised his glass in our direction. I'd expected that he'd be here because he'd said so that morning when I wanted to introduce him to the sidewalk. "Be nice. Don't even think of having another tantrum in front of him again," she muttered under her breath at me.

"Fine," I said, raising my glass and mentally wishing for direct knowledge of the dark arts so I could curse him into a toad. Wait, he already was a toad; it would have to be something different . . . a cockroach, maybe?

"What are you thinking about?"

"How much I despise certain insects," I said, taking a drink of wine.

She rolled her eyes. "Really?"

"Umm-hmm. Not kidding. Cockroaches are just vile things, slinking around into places they definitely do not belong."

She laughed at me. "You're adorable when you're jealous." She narrowed her eyes and leaned in closer. "But if you embarrass me in front of him again like you did that morning getting coffee, I will hurt you, Blackstone. And there will be lots of excruciating pain involved." She looked down below my waist.

I laughed back and only because it *was* funny, and I didn't doubt her threat for a moment, and the fact that The Cockroach was watching us from across the way. "I'll be a perfect gentleman . . . just as long as he keeps his pincers to himself."

She rolled her eyes at me again and I noticed how blue they looked paired against her dress tonight.

After dinner, I got the pleasure of being introduced to the very female, and very gracious, Alex Craven from the Victoria and Albert. I sent up a prayer of thanks to my mum that I never sent Ms. Craven the toxic text from "Ethan w/ the big knife" and figured Mum had to have been looking out for me that day. I never take my luck for granted.

It didn't take long for Brynne to be whisked away by patrons who wanted a blow-by-blow of the conserving of *Lady Percival.* I resigned myself to that eventuality and headed off to get another drink. I sensed eyes on me and turned around to find Strawberry Blonde honing in fast. *Shit.* I knew this would happen.

"Hello, Ethan. It's so nice to see you here tonight. I was just asking Ivan about you the other day."

"Is that so?" I nodded at her, desperately wishing I remembered her name. "Drink . . . um?" I looked down, feeling like an arsehole and wanting to be anywhere else at this moment.

"Priscilla."

Well, I got the first letter right. I snapped my fingers and pointed at the ceiling. "Right—Priscilla, can I get you a drink?

I'm just about to head back up to the Victorian Gallery." *Please say no.*

"Yes! I'd love a Cosmo," she gushed, her eyes lighting up as she perceived some interest on my part. She gave me a thorough looking over and I found it more than uncomfortable. This was something I'd put up with for years from women. I'd done it for the sex, of course. I mean, who will shag you if you don't at least let them admire and pretend to be flattered by their attentions? But really, I didn't like it, and it had been nothing more than a game for me. Before Brynne much of what I'd been doing had been games. *I'd been a dog.*

"And what did Ivan say about me?"

"He said you were very busy with your job and the Olympics . . . and your new girlfriend."

"Ahhh, well, he told you the truth at least," I said, looking for a way out of the room without being cruel. "I do have a girlfriend." *And I need to get away from you like right the hell now!*

"I saw her earlier at dinner. She's a young little thing, isn't she?" Priscilla stepped closer and put her hand on my arm, her voice laced with enough toxin to sting.

"She's not that young." I gulped a mouthful of vodka and prayed for some act of God to get me the fuck out of this uncomfortable situation, when in walked The Cockroach with Brynne at his side.

There's your act of God, arsehole.

"Baby." I detached myself from Priscilla and went toward Brynne. "I was just getting a drink and ran into . . . um . . . Priscilla." Bloody hell if I didn't know her last name either! This sucked, and I just didn't have the skills to do this shit anymore, not that I'd ever had them, but this was awkward as fuck.

"Blackstone." Paul Langley gave me an accusatory look. "Brynne was feeling a little light-headed and needed to take a break."

I took her hand and put my lips to it. "Are you all right?"

"I think I just need some water," she said. "I just felt hot all of a sudden and weird."

"Here, I want you to sit and I'll get you some water." But before I could move, there was good ole Langley pressing a crystal glass into her hands. I tried mental telepathy on him. *You can leave us now, Langley.*

It didn't work.

"Thank you, Paul." Brynne flashed him a grateful smile and started drinking.

"My pleasure, darling," The Cockroach purred back at her.

Damn, I'd hoped you'd left the room. Langley, the epitome of manners that he apparently was, stuck out his hand to Priscilla and introduced himself. "Paul Langley."

"Priscilla Banks. Lovely to meet you."

Marvelous. Now, can you two go off together and shag in the loo or talk behind our backs or something? Either of those would be fucking perfect.

To my good fortune, they did move away and begin a conversation. I looked back at Brynne and asked, "Feeling better?"

"Yes, much." She glanced over at Paul and Priscilla and then back to me. "Who is that, Ethan?" she whispered.

"A friend of Ivan's."

She wasn't buying it and gave me a look that spelled certain doom if I didn't come clean. "Was she a friend of yours too?"

"Not really," I offered.

"What does that mean, *not really*?"

I paused, unsure where to take this unpleasantness. A public charity event was hardly the place, but I've not always filtered my thoughts from what comes out of my mouth and therefore forged ahead anyway. "It means we went out one time together and we are not friends in any sense of the word. Not like you and Langley are friends." I raised a brow at her.

"Okay. Fair enough," she said, with a long, reflective look over at Priscilla and then back at me, before finishing the rest of her water.

Hmmm . . . so it seemed she was willing to let it drop for the moment. Thank. God. Now, if we could just escape The Cockroach and Strawberry Blonde things would be golden.

"Shall we go back up to the gallery? You must have legions of fans still waiting to talk to you."

"Right," she laughed, shaking her head. "But yeah, we really should go back. I want Lady Percival to get her due tonight. She's been hiding in the dark for far too long."

As I took Brynne up to the Victorian Gallery, I couldn't help but think she was referring to herself metaphorically with that last part: *She's been hiding in the dark for far too long.* It made me happy for some reason.

It didn't take but moments for Brynne to get caught up in another round of interviews, and I sort of faded into the background and let her do her thing. She was just starting out in her career and I wanted her to be successful for a few reasons. One, it was her dream, and two, a good job in her chosen field would keep her in London with me. I was just as motivated as my girl was.

"Enjoying the show?" Ivan's voice came at my shoulder.

"Glad you could make it tonight. We've been wondering when you'd grace us with your presence. Brynne wants to introduce you to her friend." I looked around for Gabrielle in her green dress but didn't see her.

"Brynne looks very busy right now." He glanced over at my girl admiringly. "Maybe later."

"Look, Ivan, there was a pseudo threat delivered to my office today. I'm not horribly concerned, but I want you to know the details." I handed him the envelope of photos I'd brought along, anticipating his attendance. I was a firm believer that everyone should know about the threats against them, no matter how insignificant. Crazy people never seem to get better, so everyone needs to know what could be a potential problem down the line.

Ivan and I had done this plenty of times before, so it wasn't anything new. He grunted at the photos as he flipped through them and after a minute handed the whole lot back to me. "Thanks, E, for looking out. I'm sure it'll all blow over when the Olympics are but a memory." He looked at the drink in my hand. "At least I can hope, true?"

"It's all we can do, mate." I nodded, clapping him on the back with one hand.

"I need to have something along the lines of what you're having." He waved off and left for the bar.

I nursed my vodka for a few more minutes before deciding a smoke would be just the thing. Brynne was still too busy to be interrupted, so I found Neil and told him where I was headed. I located an exit door down at street level, propped it open just enough so I could get back in the same way I'd gone out, and stepped into the cool, fresh night.

The clove tasted so fine I think I got a tad hard. Just a few more hours and we'd be on our way out of London and I'd have her all to myself. The city lights and sounds were a comfort swirled with the scented smoke that wrapped around me like a cloak. As I stood there and indulged in another coffin nail, I wondered how I'd ever get off the smokes completely. I was really trying to limit my consumption, but I'd been at it for so long, I just didn't know how to let go for good. Addiction was a powerful component of the body and the spirit. And the cigarettes had more hold on me than just the nicotine. I suppose some professional help was needed, and it was time to face up to that reality as well as some others.

I felt a vibration against my chest, and it gave me a zing because it took a moment to determine what it was. Brynne's old mobile in my front jacket pocket. The thing had been silent for so long that I'd nearly forgotten to bring it tonight, but out of habit I kept charging it and turning it on.

I pulled it out and saw the multimedia message alert. That meant a picture. I felt myself go cold and knew the frightening blade of fear slice into my gut. I pressed open and tried to breathe.

ArmyOps17 has sent Brynne a music video on Spotify.

Oh, fuck no! This is *not* happening right now. I pressed accept against my better judgment; I was compelled to look. The professional in me had to see exactly what it was. I knew the song the moment it started playing. Nine Inch Nails'

"Closer." The one that was used in the sex video with Brynne. I let it play through because I had to, but I felt ill throughout the whole song. And it was just the official music video and not the one of Brynne.

Thank. Holy. Fuck.

Images of a monkey on a cross, a pig's head twirling on something, Trent Reznor in a leather mask swinging from shackles, wearing some fetish ball gag, and a medical diagram of the female sex . . .

I pulled in a breath the moment it ended and just stared at the screen. ArmyOps17? Who the fuck was sending this shit? Oakley? My intel on him was about as secure as it could get. Lance Oakley was in Iraq and not going anywhere soon, unless it was in a body bag back to San Francisco if I got that lucky. It could happen, I reasoned.

The text came through a moment later: **Brynne, Help me; I've broke apart my insides. Brynne, Help me; I've got no soul to sell. Brynne, Help me get away from myself. Brynne, Help me tear down my reason. Brynne, Help me be somebody else. Brynne, HELP ME!!**

My fingers definitely shook as I replied to that freakish mess of words: **Who are u and what do u want from me?**

The reply was instant: **Not you, Blackstone. I want Brynne. Put out your smoke and go back inside and give her my message.**

My head jerked up and scanned the perimeter and then the rooftops. This motherfucker was on me right now?! I don't think I've ever moved so fast in my life, but I had one purpose and one only—find Brynne and get her the hell out of there.

I ducked back inside and started running. I got Neil on the headset and told him in brief to wrap it up.

"On-site security just got a bomb threat called in. They're evac-ing the whole place, E."

What? My mind was reeling with connections, but there was no time to play Sherlock. "Stay on Brynne and wait for me!" I barked.

Neil paused before replying. Not a good sign.

"Do *not* fucking tell me you aren't on her right now!"

"I think she went to the ladies, and in-house approached me—I'm going now to find her."

"Fuck!"

I changed directions and the alarm system went off. Really bloody loud. All of the exits lit up and doors started opening. Gabrielle emerged from a door just ahead of me and bolted like she was in a foot race, which was remarkable considering the heels she'd worn tonight. Her hair was all askew, and so was the skirt of her green dress as she fled.

I didn't have time to ask what was doing with her, though; I needed to find my girl. I heard pounding footsteps behind me and turned. Ivan. He didn't look much better than Gabrielle, with his hair rearranged and his shirt halfway tucked. I had to wonder if they'd been together back there . . . *I really don't have time for this!*

"Bomb threat. That's what this is." I gestured to the flashing lights. "Everyone's being evacuated."

"Are you fucking kidding me?! All this is because of me?!" Ivan exploded.

"I don't know details. I was out having a smoke when the alarm went off. Neil said in-house security got a bomb threat called in and they're closing everything down. We'll sort it later. Just get the fuck out!"

I left Ivan and ran for the Victorian Gallery. The place was an absolute crush of insanity. People shouting and running around in a panic. A lot like me.

Brynne, where are you?!

I looked for a flash of periwinkle in the crowd and did not see it. And my heart sank.

"Do you have her?" I got Neil on the headset again.

"Not yet. I've checked two different loos on that floor. Empty. I told Elaina to bring her along if she spotted her on the way out to the street where they're herding people. I'll keep checking."

In my desperation I think I would've made a bargain with the devil himself if I could just find my girl safe and sound. I headed back to the wing where *Lady Percival* was on display, hoping she might offer me a clue. I remembered Brynne saying something about access to the back room where she'd helped out when *Lady Percival* had been moved from the Rothvale over here for this show tonight. I looked for a door and there it was not ten feet down, blending into the wall— the outline of the seal, and then a small sign marked Private affixed to it.

Jackpot!

I turned the handle and pushed into a large work storage room with more doors—one of which was marked Toilet.

"Brynne?!" I yelled her name and slammed my hand hard. I tried the knob, but it was locked.

"I'm here," came a weak reply, but praise the angels, it was her!

"Baby! Thank Christ." I tried the knob again. "Let me in. We have to go!"

The door latch clicked and I wasted no time wrenching open the final barrier between me and my girl. I would have torn it off and thrown it if I'd had the ability.

She stood there looking pale, with her hand over her mouth, sweat dotting her forehead, in her beautiful periwinkle dress. The most gorgeous color in the whole bloody world right now! Maybe forever. I didn't think I would ever forget how I felt in this moment. The stark relief at finding her just about took me to my knees in thankfulness.

"What's going on with the fire alarm?" she asked.

"Are you okay?" I wrapped my arms around her, but she pressed a hand to my chest to keep a distance.

"I just threw up, Ethan. Don't get too close." She kept one hand over her mouth. "I don't know what's wrong with me. Thank the gods I remembered about this bathroom being so close by. I was in here bent over the toilet and then the alarms went off—"

"Oh, baby." I kissed her forehead. "We gotta go *now*! Not a fire but a bomb threat called in!" I grabbed her other hand and started pulling. "Can you walk?"

Her face paled even further, but she revived somewhat. "Yes!"

I fired off a call to Neil as I got us the hell out of that building.

Adrenaline has amazing powers on the human body. There are many small things to be thankful for, but the greatest thing of all was safe in my arms.

• • •

What a clusterfuck the last hours had been. I ruminated over what'd gone down as I drove into the night. Change of plans, I'd decided as soon as we got home. I called Hannah and let her know we were driving up to Somerset that night. She seemed surprised but said she was glad to have us early and that the house would be open so we could get in whenever we arrived.

Brynne was a bit harder nut to crack. She didn't feel well, for one thing, and then was worried about the bomb threat and all the paintings. So far, there hadn't been an explosion, but the whole mess was on every news station and being categorized as a terrorist risk. I would have my people investigating the bomb threat as a compulsory measure, but what concerned me far more were the messages on her mobile tonight. Whoever sent them was close by. Close enough to see me having a smoke behind the National Gallery. And if he was close enough for that, then he was too fucking close to my girl. I could hardly make sense of the text message either—just lyrics from the song typed out with Brynne's name attached to them. Gave me chills, and made my decision to get her out of the city a very easy one.

I looked over at her sleeping in the front seat, her head tilted against the pillow she'd brought along. I'd rushed her to Somerset, and I knew I'd have some explaining to do later, but thankfully she hadn't been in a mood to challenge me and went along with everything. We'd changed out of our formal clothes, grabbed the bags, and hit the M-4 for our three-hour drive to the coast.

She stirred about two hours into the drive and woke up with a direct question. "So are you going to tell me why you dragged me away tonight when the plan for weeks had been to go in the morning?"

"I don't want to tell you because it won't be nice for you to know and you're already feeling bad." I reached for her hand. "Can we wait till tomorrow to talk about it?"

She shook her head. "No."

"Baby, please, you're exhausted and—"

"Remember our deal, Ethan," she cut me off. "I have to know everything or I can't trust you."

The tone of her voice was very hard and scared the shit out of me. Oh, I remembered our deal very well, and I hated what I knew. But I also knew what I'd agreed to with Brynne. And if keeping the information from her broke us apart, then it wasn't worth the cost to me.

"Yeah, I remember our deal." I reached into my pocket for her mobile. "A message came through on your phone while I was out back having a smoke. That's why I didn't know where you were. I'd left to go outside and the bomb threat happened about simultaneous with that text message coming in."

She reached a shaky hand and took it from me. "Ethan? What's on it?"

"A music video first and then a text from someone calling themselves ArmyOps17." I put my hand on her arm. "You don't have to listen. You really don't—"

Her face looked absolutely stricken with fear, but she asked the question anyway. "Is it—is it the video of . . . me?"

"No! It's just the music video of the song by Nine Inch Nails—look, you don't have to do this, Brynne!"

"Yes, I do! It's to me, this message! Isn't it?"

I nodded.

"And if we weren't together it would have still been sent to me, right?"

"I suppose. But we *are* together and I want to keep you from having to worry about shit like that. It kills me, Brynne. It fucking kills me to see you like this!"

She started to cry. It was the silent kind of crying. The way she usually did it, and somehow the silence of her tears seemed to be screaming-loud in the car between us.

"That's one of the reasons why I love you, Ethan," she sniffed. "You want to protect me because you really care."

"I do, baby. I love you so much. I don't want you to have to see that piece of sh—"

She pressed start and the song rang out as she played the video. I watched her and held my breath.

Brynne kept it together for the whole thing, watching it through to the bitter end, in all its mad-scientist-themed fetish crap. I had no indication from her as to how she felt about seeing it, though. At least not outwardly. I couldn't possibly know.

I knew how I felt from watching her, though. Utterly helpless.

Then she got to the text message part.

"He was there? Watching you smoke?! Oh, shit!" She clamped her hand over her mouth again and gagged. "Pull over!"

Fuck! I defied the laws of physics and the road, and somehow got us off to the side. She was out and heaving in the bushes the instant the tires stopped. I held her hair away and rubbed her back. *Could this night get any worse?*

"What the hell is wrong with me?" she gasped. "Can you get me a napkin or something?"

I pulled some towels from the glove box and got a bottle of water so she could rinse her mouth. And kept my trap shut, positively sure I was having an out-of-body experience. This just couldn't be happening right now.

"I feel better," she panted. "Whatever that was tonight seems to have passed." She slowly straightened up and lifted her head up to the night sky. "Gawd!"

"I'm so sorry, baby. You're ill and I'm dragging you on a road trip and everything's so royally fucked up—"

"But you're here with me," she blurted, "and you're going to help me through whatever that shit was on my phone, aren't you?" She stared at me, her eyes still wet, her chest still heaving from being sick in the bushes, and utterly amazing to me because of her bravery.

"I will, Brynne." I took the couple steps that separated us and drew her close. She folded into my arms and rested her cheek on my chest. "I'm going to be here every step of the way to keep you safe. I'm all in, remember?"

She nodded. "I'm all in too, Ethan."

"Good. It's gonna be okay, baby." I rubbed up and down her back and felt her relax a little.

"I do feel better . . . even if I smell like puke," she said. "Sorry about that."

"That's good you feel better. And you only smell slightly of puke." I kissed the top of her head and she squeezed me in the ribs. "But we need to get off the side of the road. It's not much further, and I want to put you into a bed so you can get some rest. Freddy's a doctor. He can check you out tomorrow after you've had sleep."

"All right. One hell of a night, huh?"

"You're a fun date, Miss Bennett." I put her into her seat. "But I think I prefer staying in to going out with you." I kissed her on the forehead before I shut the door.

She laughed at that and I was glad I could still get her to smile after the cock-up of an evening we'd just endured.

"Can you smell the ocean?" I asked after we got a bit farther coastward.

"Yes. It reminds me of home. I grew up with the smell of the sea." She looked out the window. "Tell me about Hannah and her family."

I wondered if reminding her of home was a sad memory I'd just brought up, but I decided not to pry. It was something maybe for another time.

"Well, Hannah is five years older than me and bossy as hell, but she loves her little brother. We're very close . . . probably because of losing our mum at such an early age. We all just hung together very tight once she was gone. Our dad, Hannah and me."

"Sounds so nice, Ethan—how much you all care about each other."

"I can't wait for them to meet you. Freddy's a good bloke. He's a doctor, like I said before, and runs a practice in the village at Kilve. Their home is called Hallborough, an old estate out of Freddy's family—the Greymonts. These big houses on the historic registry are difficult to keep up, so they do a high-end bed-and-breakfast that Hannah runs, along with raising three fabulous kids."

"What are their names and ages?"

"Colin will be thirteen in November. Jordan just turned eleven, and my fairy princess of a niece, little Zara, was quite the surprise for everyone when she arrived just five years ago this month." I couldn't help the grin at thinking about Zara. I had a soft spot for little girls. "She is something else, I'm telling you. That little miss runs circles around her brothers."

"I can't wait to meet Zara, then. It's good to see a woman who can control all the men in her life, and at such a young age too."

"Well, you'll get your chance in the morning, because we're here."

I pulled into the gravel driveway that ran in a half circle up to the Georgian house of pale stone. There had been some mixing of architectural influences over the centuries during various remodels. The Gothic windows and points were a nice touch if you wanted historic. It was still a fine-looking house perched as it was above the coast; not bad for a seaside cottage. That always cracked me up. According to Freddy, Hallborough had been the summer cottage retreat for his family two hundred years ago when they needed to get away from Town. If this was a cottage, then what did those people back then consider a house?

"God, Ethan, this is amazing." She looked up at the façade and seemed suitably impressed. "It's gorgeous, and I can't wait for a tour."

"Tomorrow." I gathered up our bags from the back and locked the car. "Time to get you into a bed. You need sleep."

She followed me up to the side door entrance, which was unlocked, just like Hannah promised.

"What I need is a shower," she murmured behind me.

"You can do a bath if you want. The rooms are kitted out superb," I whispered as I led her up the main staircase. I knew which suite I wanted for us when I called Hannah and asked. The blue one at the corner of the west wing with the full ocean view all the way to the Welsh coast across the bay.

Brynne was impressed when I opened the door and led her in. I could tell by her expression. I think she was struck speechless as her eyes went around the room.

"Ethan! This is . . . simply stunning." She smiled wide at me and looked happy. "Thank you for bringing me here." But then she looked down and shook her head slightly. "I'm sorry tonight was such a mess."

"Come here, baby." I held my arms out and waited for her to move forward.

She practically leapt at me and I picked her up, letting her wrap her legs around me in the way I loved for her to do. I tried to kiss her on the lips, but she turned away and gave me her neck instead.

"I need to get a shower and brush my teeth before we do anything," she mumbled against my ear.

"We're not doing anything. You're going to sleep after you have your shower or your bath or whatever you're having."

"Hey." She lifted her head and gave me a look. "Are you denying me your body, Mr. Blackstone?"

I am sure it was the very last thing I expected her to ask me. "Um, why, er, no, Miss Bennett. I would never do such a moronic thing as deny you my body when you are so obviously in need of it."

"Good thing, because I am feeling much better now. *Much* better . . ." She held my face in her two hands and smiled a beautiful smile.

"Ahhh, I can see that you are."

She flexed against my cock and pulled us tighter together with her legs wrapped around me. "And I can *feel* that you are completely on board with my plan, Mr. Blackstone."

Well, of course I am when I have your legs wrapped round my arse and my cock up against a very nice part of you.

I walked us into the bathroom carefully and set her down on her feet. I found the light switch and enjoyed the second gasp out of her when she got a good look at the bathtub and the view.

"Is that the ocean out that window? Good Lord! It's so beautiful in here I can hardly stand it."

I laughed. "Now I'm not so sure if you're more interested in that bathtub or in ravishing me."

"But I can multitask just as well as you can, baby," she said, pulling her hoodie over her head and letting it drop.

"Did I ever tell you how much I love it when you call me baby?"

Her strip show was going to be so damn good I could already feel my body starting to hum all over.

"Maybe a time or two you've said so."

She pulled off her T-shirt, and that's when I saw it.

"You wore your necklace."

She nodded at me, standing there in a lacy blue bra and the heart pendant I'd given her at the beginning of our hellish evening.

"When we changed clothes I didn't want to take it off." She flipped her eyes up to mine and fingered the heart.

"How come?" I asked.

"Because you gave it to me, and told me you loved me and—"

"I don't want you to take it off," I blurted out in the middle of her sentence.

"—because you said you were all in."

"I am. With you, Brynne, I am, and I have been from the very start."

And I meant every word. I knew what I wanted. I understood it crystal clear, and there was no turning back with her now.

All in is forever, baby ...

When I reached for my girl and showed her how much I did indeed need her, and told her with words too, I knew then that the best gamble of my life had been not the cards I'd played but that one night on a London street, when a beautiful American girl tried to walk out in the dark, and I played the most important hand I'd ever been dealt and went ... all in.

About the Author

Raine has been reading romance novels since she picked up that first Barbara Cartland paperback at the tender age of thirteen. She thinks it was *The Flame Is Love* from 1975. And it's a safe bet she'll never stop reading romance novels, because now she writes them too. Granted, Raine's stories are edgy enough to turn Ms. Cartland in her grave, but to her way of thinking, a tall, dark and handsome hero never goes out of fashion. Never! Writing sexy romance stories pretty much fills her days now. Raine has a prince of a husband and two brilliant sons to pull her back into the real world if the writing takes her too far away. Her sons know she likes to write stories but have never asked to read any. (Raine is so very grateful about this.) She loves to hear from readers and chat about the characters in her books. You can connect with Raine on Facebook or visit her blog at RaineMiller.com to see what she's working on now. Please have a first look at the beginning of *Eyes Wide Open*, The Blackstone Affair, Part 3, where the story of Brynne and Ethan continues with lots of passion, surprises, and, of course, love.

Other Titles by Raine Miller
His Perfect Passion
The Undoing of a Libertine

SNEAK PEEK

_____

Eyes Wide Open

THE BLACKSTONE AFFAIR

BOOK 3

Chapter 1

Ethan's eyes held on to me as he mastered my body, his firm grip on my hips, his thick flesh filling me up and moving inside me, his mouth all over me, his teeth on my skin.

All of them gestures from the man who had broken though the walls I'd built and captured me. They were demonstrations of touch and pleasure, a means of cementing the connection between us, to keep me close to him. It was his way. He didn't need to worry though.

Ethan had me.

Despite the whole mess tonight, he had me in his arms and underneath him, his commanding strength taking charge in the way he'd done with me from the beginning. Holding me safe. That night on the street where he'd coaxed me into his car and then later with the phone calls demanding I acknowledge him, were just the start of my understanding of Ethan

Blackstone. There was so much more to the man than I ever imagined back then.

I wasn't going anywhere. I was in love with him.

"I want my cock in you all night long," he rasped, his blue eyes flashing against the moonlight as he moved. Looming over me, he plied my body in every which way as the light shined onto our naked bodies through the balcony window. Hands, mouth, cock, tongue, teeth, fingers—he used them all.

Ethan said things to me like that during sex. Shocking stuff that made me hotter than hell, nourishing my confidence, and showing me how much he wanted me. It was precisely what I needed. Ethan was my answer and he knew exactly what I craved. I don't know how he understood me so well, but he did without a doubt. Tonight had illuminated that message loud and clear. I guess I could finally admit that I was in need of another person in order to be happy.

That other person was Ethan.

I'd let someone in. The hard shell around my heart had been compromised, and very thoroughly, too. Ethan had done it. He'd worked on me, and pushed me and demanded my attention. He never gave up on me and loved me in spite of my cavern of emotional issues. Ethan did all that for me. And now I could revel in the fact that I was loved by a man whom I loved in return.

"Eyes on me, baby," he commanded on a harsh breath. "You know I have to have your eyes when I take you!" His hand had moved up to grip my hair and he tugged. He never hurt me when he pulled it though. Ethan knew just how much pressure to exert and was fully aware it sent me over

n manor fit for a king, which
ister, and being fucked to the
ome.
orgasm right now either. A girl
use myself after the second round
t I managed to wriggle out of his
the bathroom so I could clean up and
ved how he touched me all the time. I
simple and Ethan knew that. It was just
ch we were emotionally compatible.
of water and took the pill Dr. Roswell had
ne night terrors. I had a routine. Birth control
looked like something out of Buckingham Palace,
the morning, sleeping pill at night, once I was
ally sleep. I smirked into the elegant bathroom
hat bed and sleep were never synonymous when
with Ethan. We spent a great deal of time together in
t sleeping, but I wasn't complaining.
didn't expect to find him awake when I came out of the
hroom, but his eyes were open, tracking my every move-
ent as I settled back into bed. He reached for me and held
my face, something he did often when we were close like this.

"How come you're still awake? You must be exhausted after that long drive"—I paused for emphasis—"and all that superb shagging—"

"I love you and I never want to let you go," he interrupted.

"So don't." I looked into his blue eyes that seared me in the dim light.

"I never will." He said it with some hardness and I felt that he really meant it.

held on to...
Ethan knew me...
though.

"But you're going to come first!...
deep and hard, finding the sensitive spot with... to accomplish his directive.

As I felt the pressure build I let myself go to that perfect place of ecstasy, pinned beneath Ethan's body burrowed in mine and his blue eyes just inches above me. He took my mouth as the orgasm ripped into me, filling another part of me with himself, making me accept more of him, binding us together more deeply.

His orgasm followed mine within seconds. I could always tell he was close by the way he tightened to inhuman hardness right as he was about to come. The feeling was out of this world and intensely empowering. That I could pull such a reaction from him and elicit such feeling in another person did something to me. Something that healed me a little bit each time it happened—I got better inside my head all the time because of Ethan and the ways he showed his love for me. I had some hope about myself that I could be happy and live a normal life.

Ethan had given me that.

"Tell me, baby," he exhaled in a harsh whisper, but I could hear the vulnerability that accompanied the boldness. Ethan wasn't without his own insecurities, he was just a mortal like the rest of us.

"Always yours!" I truly meant my words as I felt him let go inside me.

When I opened my eyes some time later, I realized I must have dozed a bit. Ethan had rearranged us halfway on our sides but we were still joined together. He liked to stay buried inside me for a while after. I didn't mind because it was something he desired and I loved making him happy.

I just wish he'd tell me more about his dark place. He was afraid to share and while it bothered me, I mostly understood his fear. I often wondered if his reasons for needing to touch me all the time and possess me so thoroughly during sex, and afterward, too, had something to do with his time as a prisoner. *They tortured him and scarred him and hurt him.* It pained me just remembering how he'd been that night when his dreams woke him up in a panic.

I trailed my fingers over his shoulder and back. I imagined the angel wings of his tattoo and the words below them. And I felt the scars too. Ethan flicked his eyes open and pegged me hard. "Why wings? They're beautiful, you know."

"The wings reminded me of my mum," he said after a moment or two of silence, "and they covered over many of the scars."

I leaned forward, kissing over his lips with a soft touch. I cupped his jaw and decided to take the plunge. I didn't want to scare Ethan away from talking to me if he was in a mood, but figured I had to try again at some point. "And the quote? Why that one?"

He shrugged and whispered, "I think I died a little tonight."

So much for him opening up and sharing. He wasn't up for any more delving into his past. I could tell. "What do you mean you died a little?"

"When I
your mo
finger
m

of h
I neede

"I'm he
as he draped
more pleasure be

Ethan made me te
and sexy from the words
touch of his body in mine
afterward, when he held me aga

Somebody wanted me despite a
my past. Someone was willing to fight
tant to another person. To Ethan I was.
knowledge was life-changing.

Ethan's particular brand of attention was inte
lot to accept at first, but it worked for me. Ethan wor
me. He could show me how much he wanted me and for
first time I had some hope that we could really make this relationship work between us. The "let's go slow" part hadn't
happened at all like we'd agreed to when we first met, but if
we had, I very much doubt I'd be naked in bed with him at

"I love you too, and I'm not going anywhere." I leaned in to kiss his lips, the rasp of his beard stubble well familiar to me now. He kissed me back but I could tell he had more to say and could feel the edge in him which was surprising considering the orgasms he'd just pounded into me.

"The thing is I—I need something more permanent with us. I need you with me all the time where I can protect you and be together every day . . . and night."

I felt my heart begin to thud rapidly, whispers of panic taking hold. Just when I got comfortable with one aspect of us, Ethan pushed for more.

He's always been that way.

"But we are together every day now," I told him.

He furrowed his brows and narrowed his eyes a fraction. "It's not enough, Brynne. Not after what happened tonight and that fucked-up message from God knows who. I have Neil working on your mobile trace right now and we'll get to the bottom of it, but I need something more formal that tells the world you are off limits and untouchable to whatever designs they might have in regards to you."

I swallowed hard, feeling his thumbs start to move over my jaw as I tried to imagine where he was going with this. "What do you mean when you say *formal*? How formal are we talking?" Man, my voice was thready, and my heart felt like it would leap out of my chest in the next moment.

He smiled at me and leaned in for a soft, slow kiss that calmed me some. Ethan had always calmed me though. If I was unsettled or scared, he had a way of comforting me and easing the stress of the moment. "Ethan?" I asked when he finally pulled back.

"It's okay, baby," he soothed, "everything will be all right and I'll take care of you, but I know what we need to do—what needs to happen."

"You do?"

"Mmm-hmm." He rolled us over and held my face again, propped on his elbows and trapping me beneath his sculpted limbs, hard and smooth against my softer parts. "I'm sure of it, in fact." His lips dropped to my neck and kissed up to my ear and then down my jaw, over my throat, and back to the other ear. "Very, very sure," he whispered between gentle kisses. "I realized it tonight as soon as we got here and I saw that you were wearing this." He kissed over the place where the amethyst pendant he'd given me lay in the hollow of my throat.

"What are you so sure about?" My voice was faint, but every word rang out clear as a bell in the short distance between us as if I'd shouted my question.

"Do you trust me, Brynne?"

"Yes."

"And you love me?"

"Yes, of course. You know that I do."

He smiled down at me again. "Then it's settled."

"What is settled?" I implored against his gorgeous face, which had mesmerized me from the first, one side of his beautiful mouth turned up confidently, holding me firmly beneath him in a possessive hold so typical of my Ethan.

"We'll get married."